ALEX
DRAKOS 2
HIS
SCANDALOUS
FAMILY

MALLORY MONROE

AUSTIN BROOK PUBLISHING

This novel is a work of fiction. All characters are fictitious. Any similarities to anyone living or dead are completely accidental. The specific mention of known places, venues, or laws of various states are not meant to be exact replicas of those places or laws, but are purposely embellished or imagined for the story's sake.

VISIT

www.mallorymonroebooks.com

OR

www.austinbrookpublishing.com

for more information on all titles.

TABLE OF CONTENTS

CHAPTER ONE

The euphoria of the victory gave way to a quiet drive to Kari's house. Alex Drakos was behind the wheel of his Mercedes G-Wagon, but was taking call after call of congratulations and had not been able to participate in even small talk with his two passengers. Not that it mattered to Jordan or his mother. They were still caught up in the euphoria and the victory. They were still excited to be on the winning side for a change.

Fourteen-year-old Jordan Grant sat on the backseat, and he was still so excited that he was rocking side to side like Ray Charles, and even leaned forward a time or two and squeezed his mother's small arm. The second time, he spoke. "We won, Ma!" he said triumphantly, as if winning was so new to him that he thought it was a new invention. "We won!"

Karena "Kari" Grant, his mother, smiled and patted her son's hand. She understood how he felt. Winning was brand new to her, too. "Yes, we did, son," she said.

But her voice, even Jordan could tell, was far more tempered than his. Mainly because Kari was a realist and she knew that the victory they were celebrating was really all Alex's, rather than theirs, and he was just allowing them to go along for the ride. Because Kari had more than that victory on her mind. She was more concerned about the next phase of this ride. She wondered what was next?

She looked at Alex as he drove them home. Here was a billionaire industrialist. Here was a man whose corporation wasn't just a company, but a conglomerate. A man who commanded the attention of beautiful movie stars and royalty alike. But yet, on the night the town voted and approved the referendum that allowed him to build a casino and luxury hotel in Apple Valley, he chose to leave his own celebration party and drive them back home. He could have ordered one of his men to drive them (Lord knows he had plenty in town), but he didn't. He was doing it himself. That meant something, in Kari's eyes.

But what did it mean after tonight? Now that he got what he came to Florida to get, mainly that vote victory, what did that mean for their brand-new relationship? Was it over now? Would he return to New York and forget all about her? That casino wasn't going to be built overnight, and his corporation, not to mention his main home, were both in New York. Even during the campaign, when it was crucial for him to be in town to round up votes, Alex often had to fly to New York to handle his business. Were they going to have a long-distance relationship? After tonight, were they going to have a relationship at all? Winning that vote had been so all-consuming that they had never even mentioned the next step. The second act. Them!

"Let me call you back," Alex finally said to yet another caller on the other end of his phone conversation as he pulled into Kari's driveway and parked behind her old, but reliable, Toyota Tercel. He quickly got out, to open Kari's door, as Jordan, on the back passenger seat, got out, too.

"You received a lot of phone calls, Mr. Drakos," Jordan said with a grin, as Alex walked around to the passenger side of his SUV.

"Yes, I did," Alex said, with a smile of his own.

"You have lots of friends."

"A few friends phoned," Alex corrected Jordan, "but the vast majority of those calls were from vendors excited about the future. Which is good."

"Yes, it is."   Jordan knew his mother's struggling maid service was supposed to become one of those vendors once the casino and hotel were built. Alex set up and approved her contract himself. It was all good as far as Jordan was concerned.

After Alex opened the door for Kari and assisted her out of the G-Wagon, the threesome made their way to the front door. Jordan walked behind the grownups and was pleased to see that Alex was holding his mother's hand. It was eleven at night in a sleepy town. Not exactly a public show of affection. But it was enough for Jordan.

Alex's phone began ringing again as they walked to the door. He turned it off.

Kari smiled and looked at him. "A little late for that, don't you think?"

He smiled that million-dollar smile, and placed his hand to his heart. "I apologize sincerely. But there are so many others wishing to share in this victory."

Kari nodded her understanding. "It's a big deal. You should be very proud, Alex."

"It could not have been possible without your help, and Jordan's help."

Kari laughed. "Yeah, I'm sure Jordan's arrest for rape and murder and my association with Vito Visconni put those votes right over the top for you."

Alex and Jordan laughed too. Although, at the time when all of that went down, it was no laughing matter for any of them.

"I'm sure that's what sealed the deal," Kari continued, grinning. "I'm positive that's what made the margin of victory."

Alex continued to laugh as he removed his hand from her hand and placed his arm around her waist. He'd never laughed so much, or felt so deeply, until he met Kari.

When the door was unlocked and opened, Jordan congratulated Mr. Drakos again, and then took off into the house. He couldn't wait to get on Facebook and tell all his friends about his exciting night.

Alex, however, was beyond that victory. He had Kari on his mind. And more specifically tonight, after they both had had a long and grueling day, he had Kari's body on his mind. He wanted her naked in bed, and in his arms.

But Kari, as usual, Alex thought, came from out of left field. "How much do I owe you?" she asked.

He stared at her. How much *what*? But that was why he loved her. There was no one like her. "I don't understand," he said to her.

"For the repairs on your Mercedes. I see where you got the G-Wagon fixed. How much do I owe you? You were helping me, after all, when it got damaged a couple months back."

Alex smiled and shook his head. Kari owned a cleaning service, and it was a struggling maid service at that. He and she both knew she couldn't afford a doorknob on that G-Wagon. "You do not owe me a dime," he said. "I volunteered to assist. It was all on me. Don't you worry about that."

But then he moved onto her threshold, and placed his arms around her waist. "However," he added with that gorgeous smile, and Kari could tell, by that look in his eyes, what was coming next.

She smiled, too, when he didn't continue. "However, what?" she asked.

He pulled her into his arms and placed his mouth at her ear. "Why don't we go to your room and discuss it," he whispered to her.

Kari closed her eyes. It was sooo tempting! Alex did things to her in bed that no man had ever come close to being able to do. But she couldn't.

She opened her eyes and leaned back, to look into Alex's big, blue eyes. "Jordan's still up and roaming about," she said. "And I know he's a teenager who has a great idea what grown folks do when they're alone, but I can't allow that in my house. Not yet. I did that with Vito. I don't want him to think I'm going down that road again. It was too painful for him."

Alex knew what she meant. Vito Visconni was her ex-boyfriend. He was a made man for the mob she lived with when Jordan was very young. He was also very abusive.

"I hope you understand," Kari said, heartfelt.

"I do," Alex said quickly. "Please don't think I don't. I do. You will not lower your moral standards for me or anybody else, and I love that about you." His look turned more serious than lustful. "That's why I respect you so much, Karena."

He stared into her big, smoky brown eyes, and rubbed the back of his hand against her smooth brown skin. And then he kissed her. When his lips met hers, and he kissed her with a long, passionate kiss, his penis began throbbing for her. Aching for her. But he'd have her again, he knew, in time.

But as soon as Alex walked out of that door, and the door closed behind Kari, she wanted to open it back up and yell for him to come back in. And to get into her bed. She knew she was going to miss him tonight, and it was going to be lonely as hell.

But then Jordan's voice ended all hope. "*Ma*," he yelled from his bedroom, "I don't have any clean underwear for school tomorrow!"

Kari smiled, and shook her head. That was her boy! "Then you'd better put some in the machine," she said, walking away from the door. "Who do you think I am? Your *maid*?"

CHAPTER TWO

Alex turned back on his cellphone as soon as he got behind the wheel of his SUV. He had only just backed out of Kari's driveway, driven a couple blocks and turned the corner, before his phone was ringing once again. This time it was his long-time assistant, Priska Rahm.

"Oh, good," she said with a touch of franticness in her voice, "I'm so glad you decided to answer your phone, sir!"

"What is it, Priss?"

"First off, the governor of this fine state of Florida has been trying to call you to congratulate you. His office says your phone keeps going to Voice Mail."

Alex knew the governor wanted what most politicians wanted: to associate their name with a successful outcome. But although Alex campaigned mightily to secure those yes votes, he was no politician. And, now that the votes had been cast, had no incentive whatsoever to become one now. "Not interested," he responded. "Next?"

"But, sir," Priska pleaded, "we really ought to stay on good terms with the governing body of this state."

Priska really could be a pain in the ass when she wanted to be, Alex thought, and his patience with her liberties were beginning to wear thin. It was her loyalty, and the fact that he knew he could trust her, that kept her around. "What is next, Priss?" he asked.

He knew she didn't like the blow-off, but he also knew she had no choice in the matter. "Linda phoned," she said.

Alex's jaw tightened. Linda was his ex-wife. A woman who had turned his own children against him. A woman a small part of him still wanted to blame for his son's suicide, although he knew he played a far greater role in that tragedy than she ever could.

But before he could utter a single word, two SUVs sped out of the intersection he had just entered, and rammed against the side of his G-wagon: one from the driver's side, and the other from the passenger side: hemming Alex in.

"She presumably wishes to congratulate you, too," Priska was saying as Alex, knowing full well this sudden hem-in could not possibly be accidental, tossed his cellphone onto the passenger seat. When he looked at the driver on his left side, and saw him lift a gun, Alex knew he had to take corrective action and he knew he had to take it now!

He slammed on brakes so hard that the G-forces of his G-wagon caused him to nearly lose control of the wheel. It swerved from side to side by the mere suddenness of the direction shift, before it came to a complete stop. But it provided enough space for him to back away from the hem-in, and to force the two SUVs to have to turn around and face Alex.

But Alex was not about to wait on them to make the next move. He made the next move. He grabbed the pump-action shotgun he kept in the extended under-case beneath his seat, and got out of his car.

The two men in the two SUVs, who were speeding toward Alex, were astonished to see him jump out, pump that shotgun, and then fire it at the faster driver, who swerved to avoid the bullet. He didn't avoid it, he was hit in the chest, and his vehicle ended up broadside off the road.

Alex then pumped again and aimed his shotgun at the second driver, who had enough sense to hit the brakes and throw his hands in the air.

Especially when he saw Alex's security team, whose job was to stay a good distance behind Alex to ensure that no one was following him, had driven onto the side street and was speeding to where Alex stood. They jumped out of their car, too, with their weapons drawn. They were prepared for a sniper following Alex for an attempted hit. They had not been prepared for this frontal attack.

But Alex had the scene well in hand. He tossed his shotgun to one of his men, who was already aiming at the second driver, too, and made his way to the driver's car.

Alex flung open the car door, grabbed the driver by his collar, and pulled him out of the vehicle. Then Alex threw him against the SUV so violently that it dented the door.

"We were paid to do it," the driver said quickly, with his hands still in the air; with his small, beady eyes filled with that look of abject terror Alex knew so well.

"Paid by whom?" Alex asked.

"I was just trying to get paid."

Alex grabbed the driver and slammed his back even harder against that SUV. "Paid by whom?" he asked again.

"Money," he said quickly.

Alex couldn't believe it. "Is that supposed to be a fucking joke?"

"Vito," the man corrected himself. "Vito Visconni." And it was only then did Alex realize the man was not joking at all: Vito's nickname was *Money*. "Vito paid us."

Alex released the man. The last time he saw Vito Visconni he wasn't even capable of wiping his own ass. Now he was hiring killers?

"Who else did he hire?" Alex asked.

"Nobody. Just the two of us."

Alex stared at the man. In his life, he had to make snap judgments. He judged this one to be telling the truth.

But when he started walking away, he left the now hopeful driver with the naïve impression that an honorable businessman like Drakos would reward him for his honesty. And perhaps businessman Drakos would have. But Alex had a former life before he went legit. And that business was far nastier.

"Take him out, Boss?" one of Alex's men, the crew leader, asked as he approached them.

"He was paid to kill me," Alex said, frowning at his crew chief. "What the fuck you think?"

But then Alex stood next to his men and just stood there momentarily. He smiled. They smiled. But then they saw the anger in his eyes. "Next time," Alex said, "if you come late to the rodeo, don't come at all."

He gave the crew chief an even harder look of disdain, then walked away.

Alex got into his vehicle as his now overly zealous crew leader walked over to the surviving driver, and shot him at the close range. Alex drove around the scene, and then sped off. He knew his men would clean up the mess.

But he was taking no chances now. Vito Visconni might be involved. He phoned his Security Chief, and ordered him to not only put a second out-of-sight crew on Kari and Jordan, but to replace his own current crew as well.

CHAPTER THREE

"Don't you think we can do better than this?"

Kari Grant sipped coffee from her Styrofoam cup and looked at her son. It was the day after the victorious vote and she could tell he was still amped up from that victory. She knew she had to get his little fourteen-year-old brain back down to earth. They were in heavy traffic and she was driving him to school. "Do better than what?" she asked him.

"Better than this," Jordan replied. "Last night, Alex, I mean Mr. Drakos, won."

Kari smiled. "Did he really?"

Jordan grinned. "You know what I mean. We won, Ma!"

Kari was alarmed that he was still attempting to equate Alex's success as if it were their own. "Alex won, Jordan. We didn't win shit. Don't get it twisted now. What does his victory have to do with us right here and right now?"

"It has everything to do with us! We won, Ma! It was our victory, too, even though I know what you're saying. But we won too. Yet we're still driving around in your old Toyota Tercel."

Although Jordan was still grinning, his mother's look was serious. "We're driving around in our car," she said. "A car I worked my ass off to buy and pay for. And we're going to continue to drive around in this paid for car for the foreseeable future."

"But what about last night?" Jordan asked.

"What happened last night was great for Alex," Kari responded. "And maybe once the casino and hotel are built, and I'm able to get in on that housekeeping contract, it'll be good for us, too. But in the meantime, it's business as usual, Jordan. Don't forget that. Don't get caught up in all of that."

"But you're his girlfriend," Jordan said, and looked his big eyes over at his mother.

Kari still couldn't believe it herself. But it was an extremely new title Alex had bestowed upon her. They were still trying it on, the two of them, to see how it fit. But she was concerned about her impressionable son. He was behaving as if they were headed straight for matrimony, when nothing could be further from the truth. She and Alex still barely knew each other!

"I want you to promise me something, Jordan," Kari said.

Jordan didn't respond. Kari looked at him.

Jordan finally looked at her. "Yes, ma'am," he said.

"I want you to promise me that you'll never take another man's pond and call it your own."

Jordan stared at her, then took his hand and lifted it, as if it was a plane flying over his head. "That's deep, Ma. Way over my head. What does it mean?"

"God bless the child that's got his own. Depend on the Lord, and yourself. That's what it means! I made the mistake of letting a man take care of me when I met Vito. That almost cost me everything, Jordan. I'm not letting that ever happen again."

"But Vito Visconni was a jerk," Jordan said. "Mr. Drakos is nothing like that."

"It doesn't matter," Kari said, as the bumper-to-bumper traffic began inching forward a little further. "Before I met Alex I had my own thing going, and I intend to keep my own thing going. If it doesn't work out for Alex and me, and that's always a strong possibility, Jordan, then I'll still be able to stand on my own two feet and take care of my family. Namely, you. You're my responsibility, not Alex's. And I don't want you to forget that."

Jordan could see the concern in his mother's big, expressive eyes. She'd been burned before, big time, and he knew she was only being cautious now. "I won't forget it," he said.

Kari smiled at him. "I'd ruffle your hair if I didn't have this cup of coffee," she said.

"Thank goodness you've got that cup of coffee," Jordan said. "Don't touch a black man's hair!"

Kari laughed.

But as the traffic continued to move at a snail's pace, Jordan looked at her again. "Why don't you call him and say good morning to him," he suggested.

Kari shook her head. Her son was such a hopeless romantic!

"I mean it," Jordan said. "Why don't you call and say good morning to Mr. Drakos."

Kari had already thought of that anyway. "Nope," she said.

"But why not, Ma? Men like that kind of thing."

Kari looked at him. "And you know this how?"

"I'm a man. I just know it. Are you going to call him?"

The idea of her baby growing up still scared Kari. "No," she said.

"But why, Ma?"

"He knows how to call me."

Jordan smiled. "I'll bet you're going to go and see him after you drop me off at school."

"Jordan! Why do you keep harping on that?"

"But why won't you just call the man, or go and see him, Ma?"

"Because I'm not running him down. That's why."

Jordan wondered if there was more to it than his mother's general stubbornness. "He wouldn't like it?" he asked her.

"I don't know if he would or not," Kari responded. "I wouldn't like it. The last time I ran a man down and couldn't live without him and all of that bull crap did not end well for me. We both know how that turned out."

Jordan ultimately had to nod and agree with his mother. He knew. "I wish my Dad hadn't died so young." Jordan's biological father died of a heart condition. "He was a great black man, wasn't he, Ma?" Jordan said this and looked at Kari.

"He was a great man, period, Jordan," Kari said proudly. "Although, in truth, he was barely a man, really. He was only seventeen. But he was a wonderful person. He used to bring me flowers. Did you know that?"

Jordan smiled. "You told me a time or two. Or two thousand."

Kari laughed. "But it's true. A guy that young bringing me flowers? I was blown away.

Even though, one time, he brought me what he thought were flowers but turned out to be Poison Ivy and we both had to go to the hospital. But still!"

Jordan laughed happily. Kari was thrilled to see him so happy!

"We were so young then," Kari said, shaking her head. "Teenagers playing grownup games."

Then a break in the traffic. "Ah, finally!" Kari said with relief in her voice as the traffic picked up just past what was the source of the slowdown: a broke down pickup truck. Now they were off to the races, and any talk of phoning anybody flew out the window.

When they arrived at Arapaho Middle School, a private school in town, Jordan grabbed his backpack. "Am I still going to spend the weekend with Uncle Benny and Auntie Faye?" he asked.

Benny and Faye Church were not his uncle and aunt. They were his godparents. But they both were thrilled when Jordan began calling them by such affectionate terms. "You still want to go, right?" Kari asked him. "They love having you."

"Yeah, I love having them, too. We have loads of fun together. They spoil me rotten."

Kari smiled. "And that just breaks your heart, I know."

"Breaks it in two," Jordan said with a smile of his own as the school monitor, a young man, opened the car door for him.

"They still want you for the weekend. But concentrate on school today. Not the weekend."

"Yes, ma'am," Jordan said. He wanted to kiss his mother goodbye, but was too embarrassed right there around all of his schoolmates. He just glanced at her, showing affection in his eyes, and got out of the car.

But after Kari dropped Jordan off at school, she did feel some kind of way about seeing Alex again. Last night, after the county voted in favor of the referendum that would allow Drakos Capital to build a hotel and casino in Apple Valley, she refused Alex's request to go to bed with him. And she regretted that decision immediately. She wanted Alex inside of her as badly as he wanted to get inside of her. But she didn't want Jordan experiencing that. Not yet. And Jordan, to a single parent like Kari, and until he was grown and on his own, had to come first.

But she still missed Alex. And the more she thought about him, the more she was missing him. Besides, Jordan had a point. Maybe he would get a kick out of her coming by. That wouldn't be running him down. That would be dropping by to say hello.

At least, that was what she decided to tell herself.

CHAPTER FOUR

She nearly had to drive right past her office to get across town to Alex's rental house/office. But she kept going anyway. She really wanted to see him again. She really wanted to congratulate him again. She really wanted to *be* with him again. If it appeared as if he was still asleep: namely if there was no movement around the house, she wouldn't wake him. She'd keep going and take her horny behind to work. She'd feel weird for bothering to go by at all, but Kari had always been daring her entire life. It was hard for somebody like her, despite all of that *play it cool* talk she gave to Jordan, to suddenly clam up.

If she was expecting a sleepy house, she was monumentally mistaken. That house was as lively as it had ever been, with cars everywhere. It was as if the victory party from last night was still going strong. Kari had to park nearly three doors down and walk over to the house because of the glut of cars. And when she made her way up on the porch, and saw people she knew coming out with business equipment, she was shocked.

"Hey, Kari!" said one of Alex's men. "Some result last night, eh?"

"A good result, yeah," Kari said, and kept walking into the house.

"Hey, Kari," said Priska Rahm as she was packing papers into briefcases, her European accent precise. "He is upstairs."

But Kari was still trying to wrap her brain around what she was seeing. Suit cases were packed. Equipment was packed up. People were still unplugging equipment even as she stood in the foyer. "What's going on?" she asked Priska.

"We are packing up and heading back to New York," Priska said. "Our job here is done. Now it is up to the builders to make the dream a reality. But as for us? We move on to the next project. It is how Alex does business."

And that was when it hit Kari. This was temporary! There was no way an international business mogul like Alex Drakos was going to put down roots in little Apple Valley, Florida! Why would he? His business was out of New York. His home was in New York. When his casino and hotel were built, he'd visit them. Maybe a little more than a little. But he was still going to be stationed in New York. Kari was amazed how hard it hit that morning.

And it was a reality that stunned her.

"He is upstairs," Priska said again. "Would you like me to let him know you are here?"

"No, no, that won't be necessary," Kari said. "You don't even have to tell him I dropped by. I'll talk to him later."

"You are sure?" Priska asked. "I am certain he will be very disappointed to have missed you."

Kari appreciated Priska's support. They both had mutual admiration for each other. Kari knew how hard a man Alex was to work for. Priska knew how easy a man Alex was to love.

But Kari would rather not face him right now. Not when she still had to process this reality. "I'll talk to him later," she said, and headed back out of the door. She was about to walk across the porch and make her way down the steps when she heard that familiar voice; a voice sounding if it was coming from an intercom system. "Kari?"

It was Alex. She stopped when she heard the sound, and turned around. She knew he had security cameras all over the place: it was the nature of who he was that required it. The intercom thing, however, was new to her.

"Come here," his voice ordered.

She'd already been told that he was upstairs, so she assumed his voice was coming from that direction. She wanted to keep going, to deal with the reality that she was not going to be able to see Alex on any daily basis, or even close to it. But she'd been spied. She went back into the chaotic house, and made her way up the stairs.

Upstairs was off limits to his staffers, and it was like a different world up there. Alex's bedroom was directly in front of the staircase, and the door was closed. Kari gave a couple knocks first, and then opened the door.

Inside the bedroom, Alex was standing on the side of the chest of drawers fully dressed in blue dress pants, a white dress shirt, and a matching pair of blue-and-white suspenders. His clothes looked so expensive, and the material so silky, that Kari wanted to reach out and touch it. But their relationship was still new. That awkwardness was still there.

At least on Kari's part the awkwardness was there. On Alex's part, he was smiling. "Good morning," he said to her as he put on his Rolex watch and some type of diamond ring.

"Good morning," Kari responded. His smile was infectious, and she forgot about her angst and began smiling, too.

"What are you doing here?"

"I came to congratulate you again." Then she noticed his packed suit case in the bedroom, too. "Before you left town," she added.

"Thank you," he said, as he placed his wallet in his back pocket. The room smelled of aftershave and that cologne of his that she was now well familiar with. He began walking toward her. "I was going to come by your office before I left," he said.

"Oh. Okay." Then she added in a voice she hoped didn't reveal her disappointment: "I didn't know you were leaving so soon."

Alex considered her. She wore a dress he'd seen her wear before: a green and gray, form-fitting dress that dropped well above her knee, and high heels. Her hair was being worn down now, and that smile he adored was plastered all over her pretty face. She was everything he would want in a woman. And more. "Where's Jordan? At school?"

"Yeah, I dropped him off. He's going to be sorry he didn't get a chance to say goodbye."

"He'll get a chance," Alex said. They were now toe-to-toe. Alex placed his hands on either side of her small biceps, and pulled her into his arms.

He closed his eyes as her body pressed against his. There was something about Kari that made him want to hold her in a way that was equal parts possessive and protective and loving, and animal erotic. The idea that he would have to be away from her, even for a little while, was going to be difficult.

But Kari remembered what he last said. She leaned slightly back and looked into his eyes. "You said he'll get a chance to say goodbye?" she asked.

Alex nodded. "Yes. I'm going to try and get back tonight."

Kari was confused. "Tonight?"

Alex felt somewhat embarrassed, but there was no way he was staying away from Kari too long. "Yes. I have meetings all day, but then I'll get back on the plane and fly back tonight. Maybe in time for dinner with you and Jordan."

Kari smiled. "He would love that," she said.

"And what about you?" he asked.

"I'd love it, too," she said.

"You would?"

"Yes. Very much so."

"Then why don't you fly to New York with me. We'll spend time together," he added, glancing down at her breasts, "and then fly back tonight."

Kari had a business to run today. Including servicing a new client. "I think I can hold on until tonight," she said.

Alex felt a little hurt by her honest response, but that was why he loved Kari. She, unlike everybody else he knew, did not drop everything just because he wanted her to. She, unlike everybody else he knew, including himself, was a sensible, practical person.

And then a knock on his door.

Alex didn't like that. Kari could see the sudden surge of anger in his eyes. "What?" he yelled.

"Sorry to disturb you, sir, but there's an important call for you." It was Priska. All of Alex's cellphone calls, given the volume he was still receiving the day after the victory, had been temporarily transferred to the house phone so that Priska could screen the calls first.

Alex still didn't like the interruption. "How important, Priss?"

"On a scale from one to ten? A hundred. It's Reno Gabrini, sir, on line Seven."

Kari didn't know who Reno Gabrini was, but she could tell he was somebody awfully important for Priska to rank him off the charts that way. But she could also tell it by the sudden loosening of Alex's grip on her body. Maybe a part of him was still upset that she had turned him down last night?

She pulled away too. "I've got to get to work, anyway," she said.

Alex hated that they weren't able to come together again. But all of this activity in his house, and the fact that he still had tons of work to do, not to mention her own job, made it nearly impossible anyway. But they'd be together somehow today, even if he had to force the issue. "Give me a moment to answer this call," he said, "and then I'll walk you down."

"No need, Alex," Kari said with a wave of the hand. "I'm good. Take your call. We'll talk later."

Alex liked that independence about Kari too. "Okay, babe." Alex pulled her back into his arms, kissed her on her lips with a kiss that made clear he was not upset with her in the least, and then he looked into her eyes.

"Thanks for coming," he said. "It means a lot to me."

Kari smiled too. Jordan was right! Alex appreciated her dropping by. He understood it wasn't easy for her. But that was Alex, she thought. A very thoughtful man.

Besides, with all the things he'd done for her, including hiring a team of lawyers to help her son, dropping by to see him was the least she could do. And when she left his bedroom, and headed downstairs, she was glad she had had the courage to let down all of her defenses and take the plunge. Alex, she decided right then and there, was a man worth going that extra mile for.

When she left his bedroom, Alex walked over to the nightstand, pressed Line Seven, and answered the call. "Reno, good morning," he said.

And Reno, being Reno, Alex thought, came out swinging. "So your slick ass fooled those country bumpkins and wrangled yourself a casino?"

Alex laughed. "I wouldn't put it quite that way."

"But it captures the truth of the thing?" Reno asked.

Alex nodded with a grin. "It captures it, yes, it does."

"Congrats, old man! That was quite a move you made there. You're in my wheelhouse now."

Reno Gabrini owned the famed PaLargio Hotel and Casino on the Vegas Strip, a casino many considered the best in Vegas. And although they weren't besties by a mile, especially since the first time Reno met Alex was after he learned of Alex's sexual interest in Reno's wife, they shared a mutual respect for each other's success and strength.

"How does it feel the day after?" Reno asked.

"It feels great," said Alex. "It was touch and go for a while. We had to pull out all the stops."

"I know your ass did. Apple Valley, Florida. I had never even heard of it! But knowing you and your business brilliance, I'll be hearing about it soon."

"So what are you saying, Reno? Are you calling to tell me I won the bet?"

There was a bet on the table: Reno once told Alex that if Alex managed to get those yahoos, as Reno called them, to grant him permission to build a casino in their sweet little bedroom town, Reno would consider becoming a member of Alex's board of directors.

Even back then Alex knew it was bullshit. A man like Reno Gabrini, a man voted countless times as the most powerful person in Vegas, was not about to get on anybody's board. Not even Alex's. But it was Reno's expertise Alex was after.

"I'm calling to see if we can talk about it," was all Reno would commit to. "How's this weekend? Or are you going to be too busy playing that boring-ass golf?"

Alex was always booked on weekends: either with work or, as Reno aptly mentioned, playing his beloved golf. And, although Reno knew nothing about her, there was Kari now occupying a considerable amount of his time too. But could he turn down Reno Gabrini? "I can move some things around," Alex said.

"Great!" Reno said. "I'll see you then. Trina wants to talk to you also."

Trina Gabrini was Reno's wife, a gorgeous African-American woman that Alex once found sexually alluring. But she was also a woman he respected as a business powerhouse in her own right, and to whom he made a job offer. An offer Trina was still weighing and had not yet decided to take. Or, as Alex suspected, reject. "Sounds good," he said. "I'll see you guys then."

And then they ended the call.

But another knock was upon his door as soon as he hung up the call. "What now?" he yelled.

"Another must-take calls, sir," said Priska. "It's Pete."

Pete was the man in charge of Kari's security detail. "What line?" Alex asked.

"Five," said Priska.

Alex answered quickly. "Pete? Hey."

"Good morning, sir."

"What is it?"

"I sent a detail ahead of Miss Grant, to her office, so that they could get in place for their day's assignment."

"Good." That was what he was supposed to do. "But you're telling me this why?" Alex asked.

"You aren't going to believe who just walked into Miss Grant's office."

"Who?"

"Mrs. Drakos."

Alex's jaw tightened. "What in the world is she doing there? Miss Grant just left my house. She's not even there yet."

"I know. But her assistant is already there. And she walked right in."

Alex could feel his blood boil. Of all the underhanded shit Linda loved to pull. "Make sure your men keep an eye on her ass," he said. "I'm on my way."

"Will do, sir," said Pete, and Alex, angry as hell, ended the call.

CHAPTER FIVE

When Kari pulled up and saw a chauffeur-driven Rolls Royce parked in front of *Maid for Mom*, her storefront office, she wondered who it could be. Or she wondered if they had parked there in error. When she grabbed her briefcase and purse and made her way inside her office, and saw an older white woman sitting in front of her desk, she realized there had been no mistake.

The woman rose to her feet slowly when Kari walked in. Kari first glanced at Dezzamaine, her office manager. She would let Kari know immediately if this person was friend or foe. Dez, who sat behind her own desk to the side of the small office, lifted her eyebrows and shook her head. Foe if ever there was one, Kari thought.

And when she walked to her desk, and got an up-close look at the woman, she realized why. She'd seen her before, usually from her photos when she Googled her. She, Kari realized, was Alex's ex.

"You must be Kari Grant," Linda said with a smile. She extended her hand.

"Yes, I am," Kari said, shaking her hand.

The woman was staring at her hard, as if she was unable to square Kari with some image she had in her mind. Then she smiled triumphantly, as if she had decided that her mission was going to be easier than she thought. "I'm Mrs. Drakos," she said.

When she said those two words, Dezzamaine was shocked. She looked her oversized eyes at her boss as if she had just heard something crazy.

But Kari, once she had figured out who it was before her, had expected such a response. It was like all of the Kennedys, even the women after they were married, keeping Kennedy somewhere in their names. Or the Rockefellers. The Drakos name carried that kind of weight too. And this barracuda, Kari had already decided, wasn't about to give that up.

"Have a seat," Kari said as she would have said to any visitor, and walked behind her desk.

When Linda sat down, she sat down too. "How can I help you?" she asked.

"I understand you're the town's maid," Linda said as she picked lint off of her suit jacket.

Dez, out of Linda's view, rolled her eyes and shook her head. She knew what that heifer was up to.

But Kari tried to keep it professional. "I run a maid service here in town, yes," she said. "How may I help you?"

"My husband, Alex." Then Linda looked up at Kari. "I'm sure you know him, yes?"

"I know your ex-husband, yes," said Kari.

Linda smiled. "A mere technicality, I assure you."

"How can I help you, Mrs. Drakos?" Kari asked. She wasn't about to play this woman's game.

Kari exhaled. "I want to hire you, or your service as you put it, to clean a house I intend to purchase for our daughter."

Kari knew Alex's daughter had not that long ago gone to prison for embezzling from his charitable foundation. She had no idea the girl was out already. Or was she?

"How much do you charge?" Linda asked.

"I think I'm going to have to take a pass on this job," Kari said.

"What do you mean?"

"I'm going to have to decline your offer," Kari said.

Kari was surprised. "The way you're struggling to keep your doors open, and you want to turn me down? You can't be serious!"

Kari stood up. This was going nowhere. "Have a nice day, Mrs. Drakos," she said.

"I can't believe this. *You*, of all people, are dismissing *me*?"

"Yes, I am," said Kari. "That's exactly what I'm doing."

"*You*, a whore of a hood rat, are dismissing *me*?"

"Girrrl," Dez said, shaking her head, ready to get up out of her seat.

But Kari needed no assistance. And she wasn't about to let this woman cause her to lose her cool. "Have a nice day, Mrs. Drakos."

"Don't let this sophistication and class fool you," Linda said.

Where did that come from, Kari wondered. "What?" Kari asked her.

"Alex like his women with street in them, and although I'm sure I was never on your lowest of low level, I was there before. I can go back there if I have to."

Kari frowned. That did it! "Bitch, get out of my office!" she said. "Talking about street. Your ass wouldn't have lasted a day on the real street, and you know it! And cut the bullshit, okay? We both know why your ass is here and it has nothing to do with cleaning a house for baby girl. But it has everything to do with Alex. And, specifically, the fact that you don't have Alex anymore."

Dez smiled. That was the Kari she knew!

But Linda fired back. "You don't have him either!" she said to Kari. "You think you do, but you don't. Why, even the thought of it is preposterous! An uncultured, undignified, un-everything whore like you? You are not Drakos material. No way. No how."

49

"Get out of my office, and get out now, before I have to kick you out. And please let me kick you out. Please let me show you just what street looks like in the form of one of my stilettoes up your ass. Let me give your thirsty butt a taste of real street."

But then Dez caught a glimpse of movement in the corner of her eye, and then she smiled. "Have mercy," she said happily. "The cavalry has arrived!"

Both women looked at Dez, and then looked out of the plate-glassed window. Alex had just sped up and parked the car he was driving, a Ferrari, in front of the store, and was getting out quickly. Kari was always amazed by the different cars he drove. It was as is he brought a fleet along with him for his time in Florida.

She was also amazed by how fast he was moving, and by how good he looked. His expensive suspenders were now covered up, beneath a blue suit coat that fit his muscular body like a body cast. If he gained a pound, it would be too small. If he lost a pound, it would be too big. He was really a gorgeous man.

Which, Kari suspected, was the main reason why even his ex-wife was still trying to hold onto him.

Kari could see Linda attempting to spruce up her hair as Alex walked into the office. Although he was cool as a cucumber, Kari could tell, in his eyes, that he was pissed.

Linda actually smiled when he walked in. "Alexio! Hello!"

"What are you doing here?" Alex asked as he walked toward Kari's desk. He didn't look at Dez at all, which was fine by Dez. The man had business to take care of. Trash to take out. She understood.

"How have you been?" Linda asked.

"I have been fine," Alex said, although the last time he saw her she was spitting in his face at their son's funeral. "What do you want?"

"I'm here to hire a maid. That thing over there," she said, motioning toward Kari, "is a maid. A maid, Alex. You're embarrassing yourself with a *maid*!" She calmed back down. Dez was surprised he wasn't defending Kari. "Your daughter will need a place to live when she gets out."

Alex frowned. "When she gets out? Her ass just got in there!"

"The lawyers fervently believe she will win her appeal."

"Her appeal?" Alex asked. "By arguing that her dead brother was the mastermind? The brother who couldn't piss without asking her permission first?"

"The judge erred," Linda said firmly. "He would not allow that evidence to be introduced during her trial."

"Evidence? You mean he wouldn't allow those lies to be introduced at her trial."

Linda stared at him. "You want her to rot in prison, don't you?"

"I want her to pay for her crimes."

"What crimes? She stole a little money from her own father. What's the big damn deal, Alexio!"

"She stole twenty-eight million dollars from a charity, regardless of who was bankrolling it! And she has to pay."

"Do you want a relationship with her, or don't you?"

Alex frowned. "What the fuck is that your business?" he yelled.

Even Dez was surprised by that outburst. Alex was usually too cool, in her view.

But he wasn't right now.

"She's my daughter, too," said Linda.

"But what are you worrying about my relationship with her? That has nothing to do with you. And why are you here, anyway? And please don't say it's about Cate. We both know you wouldn't cross the street, let alone come all this way to Florida, for Cate."

Linda was staring at him again. Kari could see the hurt, the pain, the shame, and the anger in her eyes. "You're a cold, hateful man," she said to Alex. Then she looked at Kari. "And you want to hitch your wagon to this? I know you're desperate for money, but you're going to rue the day you ever made that decision. And children? Make sure you never have children with this monster. He'll suck the blood out of them, just like he did mine." And then she left the office, got into her car, and drove away.

Silence ensued after she left, as Alex continued to stare at her retreating car. But Kari went into the stock room in the back of her two-room office.

When Alex turned and saw that she had gone, he began to head toward the back room, too. But then he stopped, and glanced at Dez. "Good morning, Dezzamaine," he said. "I apologize for the oversight."

"Good morning, sir," Dez said. "And no problem at all."

Then Alex left.

"But you still could have stood up for Kari," Dez whispered under her breath. "Nobody else ever does."

CHAPTER SIX

In the stock room, Kari was standing at a table sorting through a big box filled with cleaning supplies. Alex walked in and sat on the edge of the desk she stood in front of, with his long legs stretched out and his big arms folded. He was now right beside her so close he could smell her sweet perfume. He could see the pain in her big, beautiful eyes.

"What's the matter?" he asked her softly.

Kari didn't say anything.

"Kari?" Alex asked. "What's wrong?"

Kari looked into his eyes. They looked so sympathetic that she suddenly felt as if she wanted to cry. But she didn't. She refused to be that weak. "I've learned something about myself," she said. "I've learned that I have an aversion to drama. And your wife? Dramaville."

"My ex-wife," Alex corrected her. "And don't worry, honey. She won't be an issue at all."

"Even when your daughter gets out? She talked as if your daughter was going to come and live here, in Apple Valley, when you aren't going to even be living here."

Alex didn't know why Kari had assumed such a thing. Not that he had any definite answers himself. He was still weighing the options.

"My daughter won't be a problem, either."

But he could tell Kari wasn't feeling it. He could tell she wasn't at all sure if he was worth the drama, however it might come. Before Kari his life was work, golf, and sleeping around. Now his life felt as if it had more meaning. As if it had more grounding. A tinge of desperation began to overtake him at the thought of losing this new lease on life. "Come to New York with me," he said impulsively. "I'll send the plane for you tomorrow night. We can spend the weekend together."

"But I thought you were coming back tonight?" Kari hated that her voice sounded so needy, but she was disappointed and wasn't trying to hide it. "You aren't coming back tonight?"

"There's been a change of plans," Alex said, hating to tell her at a time like this. "I've got to handle some business in another state, and then attend meetings in New York. And then this weekend I'm going to Vegas to meet with a couple I know. But that's why I want you to come with me. I want you to meet them too."

Kari looked at him. "But . . . I can't just pack up and leave like this, Alex," she said. "This jet-setting, last minute planning isn't my lifestyle!" she added.

"It can be," said Alex. "Tomorrow is Friday. You already told me Jordan was spending the weekend with Benny and Faye. Why not, Kari?"

Kari stared at him.

"We'll spend Friday night at my house, and then Saturday we'll fly to Vegas for a little business and, I hope, a lot of fun. I'll have you back in Apple Valley by Sunday night- just in time to tuck Jordan in for the night."

"I'm going to tell him you said that, too," Kari said.

Alex laughed. Kari smiled. Then his look turned serious, and more desperate than he would have liked to expose. "Will you come?"

Kari felt as if she was being put on the spot. But she was learning that life with a man like Alex was never going to be a nine-to-five, with every plan carefully laid out. She fought her entire life for that kind of normalcy. Was Alex worth upsetting her routine, and her life? Was this man worth the drama and the risk?

She looked into his eyes. Heck, he didn't even speak up for her when his ex-wife was ragging on her! But then even that thought upset her. When since she needed some man to speak up for her? She could defend herself. That was why she knew she had to be careful. This decision could not be about what Alex could do for her. It had to be about if she wanted to take that commodity called time, perhaps her most precious gift, and give it to him.

The jury was still out. It was still too soon. But Kari Grant was daring if she was anything.

"I'll come," she said.

And Alex exhaled, smiled, and then pulled her into his arms.

They both were relieved, and they both were uncertain.

For Kari, it was all about the heart. She didn't want to get hers broken.

For Alex, it was all about the head. Why would he pull this innocent person into his world, and his drama, and his far-from-normal life? Why didn't he leave town today, stop coming back until the casino and hotel were up and running, and let well enough alone? She'd get over him in seconds, he believed.

But that wasn't the problem.

It was him getting over her.

He didn't think he could.

That was the problem.

CHAPTER SEVEN

Linda Drakos sat in the backseat of her Rolls while her chauffeur was inside a local convenience store. She, too, was about to get out because she had forgotten to tell him to grab a box of Skittles. But just as she was about to open the door, a car pulled up beside her so close that she couldn't open the door. When she looked up, ready to cuss his ass out, she relaxed. And rolled her eyes. She knew his cool-acting ass was coming for her.

Alex got out of his Ferrari, walked around to the back-passenger door of the Rolls Royce, and got in the backseat beside his ex-wife.

"Why am I not surprised?" she asked. "You play Mister Cool around that black bitch, but Mister Angry around me."

Alex placed his hand in Linda's hand, which shocked her. But then he twisted her hand so violently that she let out a shriek and dropped to her knees on the floor of her Rolls.

"Call her out her name again," Alex said, "and I'll twist this motherfucker off!"

Linda looked at him. She knew him. She knew when he wasn't playing. "I won't again," she said. "I swear I won't, Alexio, I swear! Now stop. Please!"

Alex finally released her hand, and she breathe again. Just as she did, her chauffeur came out of the store. When he saw that she was no longer in the car, but he saw that somebody was, he quickly went to the back door and flung it open.

When he saw who was on the backseat, even as he saw his employer on her knees on the floor, his heart dropped. "Mr. Drakos, sir, excuse me, sir," he said, and closed the door back.

Linda couldn't believe it. Her bodyguard, the man paid to protect her, just closed the door back, and stepped away from the car.

Linda sat back on the backseat, rubbing her pained hand. Alex was leaned back, looking relaxed, although she knew that bastard wasn't.

Alex, in fact, wasn't even looking at her. He was staring forward, with his legs crossed. "You play games," he said to her. "You are vindictive. You are dangerous. And I know you will try this shit again, but at a deadlier level. But unlike you, I don't play games," he said to her.

He waited, as if he was expecting a response, and then he looked at her.

"I know you don't," she quickly said, realizing her error. "I know you don't play games."

He stared at her. How he ever allowed this woman to trap him in a marriage, he would never know. But he had to make sure she understood where he was truly coming from. He wasn't going to be in Apple Valley most of the time, or even in the country half of the time. He had to make himself clear. Linda was capable of anything, if she felt she could get away with it.

He leaned forward, and then leaned toward her. "Stay away from this State," he said to her. "Stay away from this town. And you had better stay away from my lady."

Linda shook her head. "*Your* lady," she said. Despite the predicament she was in, the gall of it still angered her. "You just met that woman a couple months ago, if that long, and already you're claiming her as *your* lady? It took you years to claim me. Years! You only married me because your horny ass slipped up and got me pregnant. And even after me, you never claimed any of those other hundreds of females. But she's your lady already? That plain Jane, spook, black, nigger maid?"

Alex grabbed her chin with clenched teeth, turned her face toward his, and with a knife she didn't know he had in his hand, and with a chilling look in his eyes, he sliced the side of her face.

Linda felt the cut, but couldn't believe it. She grabbed the side of her face and then looked at her hand. It was only after she saw the blood was she able to scream out. And she screamed. She couldn't believe he actually cut her. He actually cut her beautiful face! She screamed and she screamed. She kicked her feet, trying to get away from him, but he held her by that bloody hand and wouldn't let her go. Her bodyguard even looked terrified, as he could tell something was going on in that car, even if he could barely hear her cries. But he heard something. But that was Alex Drakos. He wasn't about to get in the middle of that.

"Bastard!" Linda was screaming at Alex as the blood flowed and she kept trying to get away. "You bastard!"

"I warned you," Alex said. "Now I'm warning you again." He looked her dead in her terrified eyes. His look was so terrifying that she stopped all movement to listen to him.

"You stay away from my lady," Alex said, "or I'll give you something to scream about."

Their eyes locked onto each other. Then Alex reached up his hand to touch her sliced face. She moved her face back in terror. He smiled. Linda couldn't believe it. That sadistic bastard actually smiled. And then he grabbed a handkerchief out of his pocket, wiped her blood off of his hand, and got out of her Rolls.

He got in his own car, backed up, and sped away.

It was only after he was completely out of sight did her bodyguard get onto the backseat.

Linda was still holding her bleeding face, and crying.

"He cut me," she said. "Your coward ass let him cut me! You let him cut me! Now what are you going to do about it, Jake?"

What did she expect him to do? "Go get some Neosporin?" he asked.

She took off her high heel and angrily threw it at him. He ducked. "Drive you piece of shit!" she yelled. "Drive!"

And the bodyguard hurried onto the front seat, and drove.

CHAPTER EIGHT

Kari folded another pair of panties and placed them into her suitcase. Jordan, lying across her bed, smiled. "Dang, Ma!" he said. "It's only for the weekend. How many pair of drawers do you have to take?"

Kari could feel her face blush. She knew how often Alex liked to have it, and she knew she had to be prepared to change underwear a lot. But she certainly didn't want her fourteen-year-old son to know that! "Don't you worry about what I'm packing," she said. "Don't you have homework to do, anyway?"

It was Thursday night. "I did it already." Then he smiled. "This time tomorrow night you'll be on your way to New York to spend the weekend with Mr. Drakos, and I'll be with Uncle Benny and Auntie Faye."

"And you'd better be on your best behavior, too, boy," Kari said. "They better not give me any kind of a bad report."

"They won't."

"They better not."

"Where's Mr. Drakos anyway? Why is he always out of town?"

"What do you mean out of town?" Kari asked. "He lives in New York."

"That's where he is now?"

"Why?"

"I was just wondering."

"He's handling some business, that's all I know. He doesn't go into those kind of details with me, and I don't ask him to."

"Why not?" Jordan asked. "You're *scarred*?" Jordan smiled as he purposefully mispronounced the word scared.

Kari smiled too. "No," she said, "but he's entitled to live his life."

"Are you living yours by going to New York just because he asked?" Jordan asked.

"I want to go, if that's what you're asking."

"What are you guys going to do all weekend?"

"Okay, enough questions," Kari said. She had a great idea about one thing she and Alex were going to do all weekend. "Go find something to do," she said.

Jordan smiled as he got off of her bed. Then he looked at Kari. "I heard his ex-wife came to town," he said. "Is that true, Ma?"

Kari wasn't going to lie to him. "Yes," she said.

"Is she moving here or something?"

Kari shook her head. "I doubt it." Then she exhaled. "Don't worry about her, Jordan. Alex can handle her."

"What about you? You can handle her?"

"Child please," Kari said as she continued to pack. "Can Lebron James handle a basketball?"

Jordan laughed, and felt better as he left her room.

The EMT loaded the gurney onto the back of the ambulance, and got back out. Vito Visconni, paralyzed from the neck down, laid on that gurney waiting to be transported. It was his first day out of the hospital, and he was being transferred to a nursing home for rehab. Why they felt a need to rehab a man the doctors already said would never walk again was insane to Vito. But at least it got him out of that hospital.

But when a man, fully dressed and wearing gloves, got into the back of the ambulance with him, and the EMT was nowhere to be found, Vito became concerned. When the man looked up, and Vito saw that it was that fucker Alex Drakos, Kari's new man, he nearly jumped from that gurney.

"Wait a minute," he said. "Wait a fucking minute! What are you doing here?"

Alex closed the door of the ambulance and took a seat beside the gurney.

"No, wait!" Vito yelled. "What are you doing here? You aren't supposed to be in here!"

Alex hit the roof of the ambulance, and the driver began driving away from the hospital.

Vito cut the hysterics. He knew the game. He'd been a wise guy most of his life. Alex had obviously paid off those hungry EMTs and had his man behind the wheel. All of that crying foul didn't mean shit now. "What do you want?" he asked him.

Alex leaned back, crossed his legs, and just stared at Vito.

Vito frowned. "What are you looking at? I know I look good." Then he paused, and stared at Alex. He knew how to get a rise out of him. "How's Kari?" he asked.

Alex remained silent.

"Cat got your fucking tongue? I asked you a question."

Still no response.

"I don't know what she sees in you with your fancy clothes and women. What you want with Kari and that bigmouth boy of hers? She ain't your speed and we both know it! She ain't glamourous. She ain't even all that good looking. Why some dude like you want her?"

Still no rise out of Alex.

Pain gripped Vito's chest. Tears appeared in his eyes. He laid his head, the only part of his body functional, back down. "I miss her," he said. "If she would have just come back to me when I got out of prison, none of this would have happened. Why she had to act like that? Everything would have been so different if only she would have . . ."

He shook his head as if he wanted to shake off the emotions. "You know why I wanted Kari back? Hun? You wanna know why?" Although Alex didn't answer, Vito proceeded as if he had. "I wanted Kari back, not because I was all in love with her and was all attracted to her. I wanted Kari back because she was my lucky charm. I had my best run of luck when I was with her. Hands down. As soon as she left me, I get picked up by the Feds!"

He shook his head again. "Kari's got something that none of them bitches I was fooling around with ever had. She's a woman a man can rely on. I could trust her and depend on her. I knew she wasn't gonna be cheating on me or lying to me or stealing my dough. That's why I wanted her back." More tears appeared in his eyes. "She was my lucky charm, man. I knew if I didn't have her with me, I wasn't gonna make it. Now look at me. I was right."

Alex understood exactly what he meant about Kari. She was his lucky charm too, and so much more. But Alex was greatly unimpressed with Vito's sob story. "Why did you hire those men to kill me?" he asked him.

Vito was so shocked to hear him finally speak that he, at first, just looked at him.

But when Vito clammed up, Alex grabbed Vito by his neck and squeezed hard. "This motherfucking head is all you've got. Answer me or you won't even have this big-ass head anymore."

"Okay, okay," Vito said, giving in quickly.

Alex stared at him. "You used to want death. When you were first hospitalized, you used to beg to die. Now? Not so much."

Vito got his second wind. "The only thing I want dead now is the bastard who paralyzed me," he said defiantly. "Since you're that bastard, why wouldn't I want your raggedy ass dead? What do you think?"

"You want to know what I think?"

"Yeah, motherfucker. Yeah. What do you think?"

"I think," Alex said, as he moved closer to Vito and placed him in a headlock, "is that you should have quit while you was a head."

And then he twisted Vito's neck until he broke it.

And Vito was dead.

CHAPTER NINE

Faye and Benny Church were in the front seat, with Benny behind the wheel, while Kari and Jordan sat in the back. It was Friday evening, Kari had agreed to meet Alex in New York, and they were driving her to the airport. But it was all so surreal to her two closest friends.

"A private plane," Faye said. She was a gorgeous black real estate broker married to a gorgeous black attorney, but Alex, and his billions, was from another planet to them. "You are about to board a private plane that was sent here by Alex Drakos himself for the expressed purpose of picking you up."

Jordan grinned. "That's how Mr. Drakos rolls," he said.

Benny looked at Jordan through the rearview and laughed.

"But that's something else, girl," Faye said. "You went from how are you going to pay your bills, to a private plane!"

"I'm still trying to figure out how I'm going to pay my bills," Kari pointed out with a grin. "And this is Alex's plane. Not mine."

"She doesn't have to struggle," Jordan said. "Mr. Drakos gave her a credit card to use any way she wanted. But Mom won't use it."

Kari frowned. "What I look like using that man's card, Jordan? If things go south with Alex and me, I'll owe him all that money back."

"No, you won't."

"Yes, I will."

"According to Judge Judy show," Jordan said, "if it was a gift, he can't change it to a loan if y'all break up."

Benny laughed. "The kid is right!"

"According to my conscience," Kari countered her son, "if things go wrong between Alex and me, I'll owe him that money back. And I wouldn't be able to afford to pay it back."

"Then why did you accept the card if you weren't going to use it?" Jordan asked.

"I'll tell you why," Faye said, "because I know your mama. She took that card just in case she had to use it. Because ba-by, she'll use that sucker in a heartbeat if it'll keep the doors of *Maid for Mom* open! She'll pay every dime back, but she's no fool. She'll use it if she has to. I know your mama."

"But your mother is right to be cautious, Jordan," Benny said. "You don't want her beholden to any man. You want her to be independent, like your aunt Faye. If I left your aunt tomorrow, she'll be just fine."

"Darn right I will," Faye said with a smile.

"That's why I'll never leave her," Benny said. "She'll be too fine and these men will line up to take my place!"

"Darn right they will," said Faye.

"See," said Benny, as he looked at a smiling Jordan through the rearview.

They arrived at the airstrip where the big private jet was waiting, with the crew chief standing at the foot of the stairs to escort Kari onboard. It was a gorgeous aircraft and all of them were impressed. Including Kari and Jordan, who had flown on it before.

But as soon as the car doors opened, and Kari, Jordan, and Benny and Faye got out, two cars drove up that they didn't realize had been behind them, and security guards got out.

"Who are they?" Faye asked.

"Mr. Drakos's men," Jordan said proudly. "They protect us when he's not around. We just never are supposed to see them. And we don't."

Benny and Faye looked at Kari. They couldn't believe how much Alex was pulling out all the stops for her.

But while Faye and Jordan found it enchanting, Benny found it concerning. Alex was known the world over as the playboy billionaire. That was his nickname! He knew how to wine and dine women with the best of them, and only did it because he could. They, in Benny's mind, could be reading too much into Alex's generosity.

But when he looked over at Kari, whom he viewed as his kid sister, Kari smiled. "Don't worry, Benny," she said. "I know all of this is more Alex being Alex rather than Alex being into Karena."

Benny smiled. Kari was a well-grounded woman. What in the world was he worrying about?

CHAPTER TEN

Drakos Capital was a massive conglomerate within its own massive building in downtown Manhattan. Alex's office was on the top floor, and he sat behind his desk, on his computer, reviewing the specs of one of his newer endeavors: Franchise Hub. But Alex also knew that if Kari were to see this office, he knew exactly what she would say. "This office is bigger than my entire house!" she'd declare. It would be an exaggeration, but Alex smiled just thinking about her and her genuineness.

"Knock knock." Matt Scribner, Alex's chief financial officer, walked in. "Got a minute?"

"What's up?" Alex continued to review his specs and didn't bother to look up.

"Tired, if you can call that up."

Alex smiled.

Matt sat down in front of Alex's desk. "I just completed my pre-build financial assessment on the Apple Valley project."

Alex looked up for that. "And?" he asked.

"All systems are go. The financials for every builder looks good. There were no red flags. No projected cost overruns. At least not yet."

Alex grinned. "Give it time."

"Agreed," Matt said. "But for right now, we're great. That casino and hotel is going to set that region of this country on fire."

"That's the goal."

Then Matt remembered something. "Have you been able to rope Reno Gabrini in yet?" he asked.

"Not yet. I meet with him this weekend."

"If we get his expertise, there's no way we can lose. He runs the PaLargio like a well-oiled machine. I've never seen anything like it. It'll be great if we can get him on board to help us."

But Alex had something more pressing on his mind. He leaned back. "I want to build a house in Apple Valley," he said.

Matt was surprised. "A house? For who?"

Alex looked at him. "For me."

"For you? You mean until the project is complete? But even still, you've never been that involved with the nuts and bolts of a project before. You've never been involved with the nuts and bolts at all! What gives?"

"I want to build a permanent residence in Apple Valley."

Now Matt was floored. What in the world? Everything he knew about Apple Valley was that it was a nothing town on the Florida Panhandle that the Drakos casino was going to turn into the *it* place to be in the south. But the idea that Alex Drakos, Mister Metropolitan, would live there? Ridiculous, Matt thought. "Why?" he asked his boss.

Alex answered to no one, and especially not his CFO. "Have the architects draw up blueprints. Tell them my only requirement is that it is family friendly. Basketball court. Tennis court. Game room. Pool."

"Golf course?" Matt asked.

Alex smiled. Everybody knew about his obsession with playing golf, although he hadn't bothered in weeks. "That too, yes," he said.

But then his wandering eyes wandered over by the clock on the wall. And he was shocked. "Is that time right?" he asked. He quickly looked at his wristwatch for confirmation while Matt turned toward the clock to see what time he meant.

When Alex confirmed that the time was indeed right, and before Matt could say a word, Alex was on his feet and grabbing his suit coat off of the back of his chair. "I've got to run," he said.

"Run where?" Matt asked, rising too. "I thought we were going to discuss the Corcoran project."

But Alex was hurrying out of the door without bothering to discuss anything more. He was gone.

CHAPTER ELEVEN

A half-hour into her flight and Kari Grant was relaxed. Earphones in her ears, listening to her music, and her phone in her hand reviewing her emails. Her head was bobbing and her face was smiling: she felt good. Jordan was in good hands with his godparents, and she would soon be in good hands, she was certain, with Alex. She didn't realize, however, that the crew chief had been attempting to get her attention, without touching her, for several seconds until she finally glanced up, and saw him standing there.

She immediately removed one of the earplugs from her ear. "Hi," she said.

"Hello," said the head of the flight crew. "I was wondering, ma'am, if there was anything you needed?"

"Oh! No. Thank you. I'm good."

"My staff has been attending to all of your needs?"

"Completely, yes."

"If you have any concerns whatsoever," the crew chief said, "and I mean *any* concerns, please do not hesitate to let me know and I will correct the situation immediately."

Kari smiled. "I will. Thank you."

And the crew chief left her alone.

Kari leaned back and shook her head. This must be what it felt like, she thought, to live a dream. She remembered on her very first date with Alex, and how he wanted to fly her to New York for dinner without even mentioning anything about leaving town until they were at the airport. She was scared to even get on his plane that night. Now she was not only on his plane, but she was gladly going to New York to spend the weekend with Alex. Just the two of them. For a girl like Kari, who used to always find herself waiting for that break in the weather when that rain called life would always keep on pouring, she wasn't sure if it could get any better than this.

She put back in her earplug. Nodded to the beat. And determined within herself that she was going to forget about the job, stop worrying about Jordan, and enjoy her weekend for once in her life.

Kari Grant was happy.

She didn't realize just how happy she truly was until the plane touched down in New York and she looked out of the window. She expected a limo to be waiting. Alex, she knew, wouldn't have it any other way. If he said he was going to do something, he was going to do it in style.

But when Alex himself got out of that limo, buttoning his suit coat, looking every bit that gorgeous specimen of man she could hardly wait to get her hands on, it was only then did she allow herself to not just be happy, but to get giddy with it. She started grinning and shaking her body from side to side. He told her that he would be tied up at the office and would see her later tonight at his house. But he showed up to meet her plane anyway. That was a good thing.

But Kari was no idiot, either. She knew he probably pulled out the stops for every woman he ever dated. But the fact that he came to meet her plane, rather than sending one of his assistants, as he said he would, said a lot about where he saw their relationship. They were moving, she felt, in the right direction.

And when she began walking down the steps of the plane, and Alex began walking toward the plane with a faster gait than was normally his stride, her excitement increased tenfold. She felt as if she had been off to war or something, but was now back home. To sleep in. To relax. To be with the man she loved!

She caught herself. *Love already, Kari? Really? You've only known the man for a couple months and you're all in love?* She wasn't going to call it love, but when she stepped off of that last step, and Alex's gait had increased even more, it sure felt like love.

It felt so much like love that she had to talk herself down. Stay cool, Kari, she said to herself. Don't go running to him like some giddy fool. Every time you saw that man you were always running to him as if you were some tail-wagging puppy. Stay cool. Let him do the running this time!

But Kari didn't have a fake bone in her body. She was going to be Kari. And that was why, as soon as her feet hit the ground, she was off and running.

Alex grinned broadly when she began running to him. He loved her enthusiasm! It made him feel a way he'd only been able to feel with Kari: it made him feel special.

And, to the utter shock of his own men, his driver and bodyguard, he started running too! They looked at each other. They knew the boss liked that black girl from Florida. They knew he liked her maybe even above any of his other girls. But damn. They'd never seen him like this!

Alex never cared what other people thought, and was too old to start caring now. His life was a dark, depressing hole before he met Kari. He worked. He golfed. He slept around with woman after woman who meant nothing more to him than a sex toy would. Now his life felt fulfilling and worth the effort. Now he had a reason to get out of bed. Yeah, his ass was running, he thought. He didn't care who saw him, or how unsophisticated it looked. Kari was in town and he couldn't wait to hold her. He didn't give a shit who was watching, either.

And when their running bodies collided, he placed his arms around Kari's waist, and hoisted her into his big arms. She wrapped her legs around him and they kissed, right then and there, as if they were kissing in bed. Which, Alex knew, was exactly where he was taking her next.

And when they got into the limo, sitting so close they were shoulder-to-shoulder, it was Alex's enthusiasm that wasn't lost on Kari. He even held her hand.

"So," he said, as he slouched down in his seat and leaned his broad shoulder closer against her small shoulder, "how's life in Apple Valley since I left?"

"Boring," Kari said.

Alex laughed. "Good," he said.

"But for real," Kari corrected herself, "It's been okay. Just busy as usual. What about life in New York since you've been back?"

"Boring," he said and they both smiled. Then he added: "You weren't here. What do you think?"

Kari laughed. "Yeah, right. The city that never sleeps boring just because I'm not in it? Yeah, right," she said again.

Then her cellphone rang. When she pulled it out and looked at the Caller ID, she didn't hesitate in answering. "Hello, Dezzamaine. Hello lady with the most countrified-ass name in America." Although the phone wasn't on Speaker, Alex could hear Dez laugh over the phone.

But while Kari crossed her legs and listened to her devoted secretary, Alex glanced down at those legs. She wore a long-sleeved white, cotton, button-down blouse, and a form-fitting powder blue skirt that dropped just above her knees, and the sight of her thighs caused his dick to throb. Whenever he was with Kari, she became wetter faster than any woman he'd ever been with. Sometimes all he had to do was rub her very gently, an procedure he was looking forward to. He leaned his head back, and squeezed her hand.

But Kari was totally focused on that phone call. Finally she replied to all she had been hearing. "What do you mean it bounced?" she asked into the phone. Alex didn't look at her. She was entitled to her privacy. But he listened carefully to that call.

"The check bounced," Dez, on the other end, said to her boss. "There were insufficient funds, and it bounced."

"Oh, geez!" Kari said. "I forgot to move it from my savings! Wait a minute."

Kari quickly went to her bank's mobile website on her phone, transferred money from her ever-dwindling savings account into her business checking account, and then pressed Send.

"Okay, it's done," she said to Dez. "Give it a few minutes and then try again."

"Will do, Boss. But I still don't know why you just don't link your savings account to your bank account to avoid these problems."

"My bank won't let me link a business account with a personal account."

"You need a new bank."

Kari nodded. "I agree."

"Bye, Boss. And thanks!"

Kari thanked her for handling the situation, and the entire business while she was gone, then ended the call. "Sorry about that," she said to Alex.

At first, Alex said nothing. Kari looked at him. Then he spoke. "You have not used the card."

Kari could tell he didn't like the fact that she hadn't used the card, a card he gave to her for moments like this. "No, I haven't," she said.

"You prefer to suffer?"

She attempted to smile. "I'm not suffering."

"Then what do you call it," Alex asked with edge in his voice, "when checks are bouncing and you're forced to move money from here to there?"

"That was just a mix-up, Alex. It's not an everyday thing."

Alex nodded. "You prefer to suffer."

"I don't. But . . ."

"Go on."

"Look, Alex, you've already done too much for me. Benny told me how you paid him thousands of dollars for his legal services when Jordan was arrested. I can only imagine how much you had to pay those high-powered Miami lawyers and investigators and all those other people who worked that case. It had to be a fortune. You did what I could never have done: you saved my son from what was certain to have been a long time in prison. I'm eternally grateful to you for that. But my cleaning service? That I can handle. I got that, Alex. I promise I got it."

Alex stared into her eyes. He'd never met anybody like her. They hugged. Then Alex reached over and placed his hands between Kari's legs, squeezing her vagina over her panties, causing her to laugh. "I miss that," he whispered in her ear.

Kari reached over and squeezed his penis, causing him to grin, because she missed that too.

CHAPTER TWELVE

His mansion was quiet. It would have been quiet enough to hear a pin drop. But even from downstairs, the soft sound of bedsprings creaking could be heard. But the further up the staircase, and around the corridors that led to the master bedroom, those soft sounds became louder and louder. Until Kari screamed.

Alex's hand was on her throat as they were knelt, naked and sweaty, in the middle of the bed. Alex was knelt behind Kari, and his thick cock was deep inside of her from the back, and her ass was pushed against him. He was pumping and pumping into her. He was pumping fast, and then slowing down and rubbing her hips when the sensations were overrunning him, and then he was pumping her ass fast again. He was plowing into her. He had never wanted another human being's sex the way he wanted Kari's.

And Kari could feel every inch of his dick inside of her. And whenever he squeezed her throat with one hand, and squeezed her breast with the other hand, she screamed out with a shout that even unbridled joy couldn't contain. Kari felt free with Alex. And that liberty heightened her arousal.

Alex was aroused too. He was going all out. He was giving to Kari the kind of fuck that had him pumping so hard into her that they both lost their balance and fell onto the bed.

Alex's cock had fallen out of her wetness when they fell, but it only gave Alex the opportunity to kiss her ass with hard, deep kisses, to slide his tongue between her crack, and then to get back inside of her even deeper than either one of them thought possible. And he was pounding her again.

They fucked for nearly forty minutes that way. Fast and slower. Harder and softer. Until he pushed in all the way one time too many, and they couldn't do it anymore. They had been getting to the brink of cum, but Alex had been easing back up, slowing back down, so that they could continue the joy of the ride.

But that last push-in did both of them in. And they couldn't ride anymore. They came. They came with an outpouring that neither one of them would ever forget. It was the hardest cum that even well-traveled Alex Drakos had ever experienced. His entire body felt as if it could explode, as he poured into her.

Her eyes opened in a room that still was not familiar to her. And that unfamiliarity initially scared her. When she realized she hadn't been kidnapped by aliens but was actually in her lover's bed, she quickly turned over to feel the comfort of that lover. But he wasn't there.

Kari didn't panic. This was Alex's house, after all, and she felt secure with him. She just had to find him.

She threw the satin sheet off of her naked body, grabbed the first thing she saw, which was her own white, button-down cotton shirt, and made her way out of the bedroom. Although her shirt covered her butt, it barely covered it, and she felt naked and alone going down his winding staircase. Alex didn't just live in a house, after all. He lived in a historic mansion on the Hudson River, in a neighborhood where people with names like Rockefeller and Rothschild undoubtedly called home. And what about his servants? Were they lurking around? It was late at night, but still. Alex had a full staff, and those were only the ones she knew of, who lived on the grounds.

But by the time she made it downstairs, and she had not run into any servants, she felt better. She relaxed completely when she smelled food. She made her way into his gourmet kitchen.

Alex, in his bathrobe, was standing at the center aisle slicing and dicing away. Kari smiled to see him appear so domestic. "Cooking?" she asked as she went and stood beside him.

"You've got to eat," he said. Then he smiled that roguish smile she loved. "I ate already."

At first, she was surprised that he would have eaten without her. But when he gave her that sly look, which made clear that the eating he meant was between her legs, she bumped him with her body and shook her head. "Quit playing, boy," she said. Then she asked: "What are we having?"

"Fasalada."

Kari smiled. She'd never heard of it. "Greek, I take it?"

"Of course," he responded. "It's a delicious bean soup that will also be loaded with veggies."

To say that Kari was less than excited would be an understatement. "A bean soup, hun?" she asked.

Alex laughed. "You'll love it, darling, don't worry!"

Kari smiled, too, and went around the island and sat on one of his fancy stools with a round, crystal back. She leaned back. Alex looked at her. "It's good to have you here," he said. "It's good to have movement in the house, late at night, other than my own."

"Oh, come on, Alexander. Surely you have had other females pattering around in this big house late at night before."

But Alex was shaking his head. "Nope," he said, as he looked back at his food and continued to chop away.

But Kari was confused. "Nope what?" she asked.

"You're the only one."

Kari stared at him. "I'm the only one what?" she asked.

"Who's ever stepped foot in my home," Alex responded. "I have taken women to my apartment in Manhattan, yes, I have. Many times. And to other places that I own. But never here."

Kari frowned. "But you were married, Alex."

"We never lived here. This home I acquired after I divorced Linda. It was a celebration gift to myself."

Kari smiled.

But hearing Linda's voice reminded him. "She won't bother you again," he said.

Kari was still processing what he had said about no other love interests ever in his home. That she was the first. And only. It was a magnificent shock to her.

But then she heard what else he said. "Who won't bother me?" she asked. Then she realized who he had to have meant. "How do you know that?" she asked.

"After I left your office," Alex said, "I had a talk with her."

"In Apple Valley?"

"Yes."

"What about?"

"The disrespect she showed to you." Alex looked at Kari. "And how that will not be tolerated. Not by her. Not by me. Not by anyone."

He and Kari stared into each other's eyes. Were they entering the proverbial next level of their relationship without having verbalized what they were doing? Did Alex feel as strongly about her as she was feeling about him? She thought he didn't stand up for her that morning when his ex-wife showed up at her office. She should have known that he wouldn't stand for that and would handle it in his own, calculating way.

"Thanks," she said to him. "I don't know what you did, but I'm sure you put fear in her heart."

"And on her face as well," Alex said.

Then Alex continued to chop veggies, as what Kari could only describe as a regretful look came over his own face, and then he tossed those vegetables into his wok.

But Kari could tell something else was on his mind. His brows, for one thing, remained knitted. "What is it?" she asked.

He began stirring the food, and then he spoke. "These people we are going to meet tomorrow in Vegas is a casino mogul and his wife."

"Really? Okay." Then she smiled. "You're the only mogul I've ever met. At which casino is he a mogul? Would I have heard of it?"

"If you've heard of the PaLargio," Alex said, "then yes, you've heard of it."

Kari couldn't believe it. Her eyes stretched. She spoke in syllables. "The *Pa-Lar-Gi-O*? I'm going to meet the owner of the PaLargio Hotel and Casino? The one on the Vegas Strip?"

Alex smiled. "That's the one."

Kari smiled too. "Wow, Alex. That's a big damn deal." But despite her smile, Kari was already feeling uneasy about meeting such a powerful person. "To say the least."

But Alex's eyebrows remained knitted. "His wife," he continued, "is Trina Gabrini. I offered her a job as the CEO of one of my companies. A startup."

That sounded odd that he would tell her that. She looked at him. "Did she accept your offer?"

"No. Not yet. I suspect she will not."

"Why not?"

Alex didn't respond. And Kari sensed why. "Is she, is this Trina Gabrini, a former girlfriend of yours?"

"No."

But Kari continued to stare at him. "Did you want her to become a girlfriend of yours?"

Alex hesitated, but answered her honestly. "Yes."

Kari could feel a slight drop in her upbeat spirit. "Why didn't it pan out?" she asked him. *And why are you telling her this now*, she wanted to ask.

"She was married," Alex said. "And meant it."

Kari's heart dropped. He obviously still had a thing for this woman. Why else would he bring it up?

"I wanted you to be fully aware," Alex said as if he heard her thoughts.

"Aware of what?"

"Aware that it was an attraction that went nowhere and that is now over. I am telling you about it because I want no secrets between us."

If that was the real reason, Kari could appreciate that. Everybody, after all, had a past. Even her. She nodded her head. "Thanks for the heads up," she said.

"Speaking of heads up," he said as he finished wiping his hand on the cloth, "come and give me some."

Kari smiled, but rose from her stool. "Do you ever get tired of fucking, Alex?"

"Tired of fucking you? Hell no!"

Kari laughed. But when she made her way up to him, and he opened his robe, revealing a fully aroused penis, the laughs were over.

Kari gladly knelt down, and pleasured her man.

But just as he was about to cum, and she thought her work was done, he lifted her onto the island, opened her legs, and had himself a second fulfilling round. On her.

CHAPTER THIRTEEN

Reno Gabrini tossed the thick file onto his messy desk and angrily leaned back. "What the fuck you think this is?" he asked his Talent Manager. "Does it look like I'm running a fucking carnival? I've already got thirty-five circus acts. Thirty-five! More than any other hotel on the Strip. I tell you get more talent for the new wing, and what do you do? You hand me a proposal filled with twelve more! Twelve more circus acts. Are you fucking kidding me?"

"I understand what you're saying, Boss," the manager said. "But those acts are the ones bringing in the crowds."

"Bullshit! Caesar's Palace has Celine Dion and Elton John. The Wynn's getting Mel Brooks for crying out loud. But I have fucking clowns and elephants and lions and tigers and bears! And it's my numbers that are down this quarter. Not theirs!"

One of Reno's assistants walked into an office already filled with managers and other assistants on phones, computers, and anything in between. She walked over to his desk. "Excuse me, sir," she interrupted.

Reno looked at her as if she'd just lost her mind. "What are you doing? You see us talking here?" He was from Jersey, and that accent had never left him.

"I apologize for the interruption, sir," the assistant said, "and I don't mean to but in."

"Then but the hell out!"

"Yes, sir. But Mr. Drakos has arrived, sir."

The assistant inwardly smiled when she saw the change in her boss's bombastic attitude.

And Reno nodded. "Got it," he said. Then begrudgingly added: "Thanks. Then he rose to his feet and put on his suit coat jacket. He looked at the man who still stood before him. "Take those shit acts in that file and find me some real talent," he said, "or I'll find me a real talent manager."

"Yes, sir. Don't worry, sir," the manager said, as Reno left the office.

When he left, the assistant looked at the manager. "If I had a dollar for the times he's threatened to fire you," she said, "I'd be rich."

But it was no laughing matter to the talent manager. "Fuck you," he said angrily, as he grabbed his thick folder, and left.

The assistant, well accustomed to the pressure he was under, still couldn't help but laugh.

CHAPTER FOURTEEN

He found him in the crowded casino. At the blackjack tables. As Reno walked toward him, he noticed a black lady cheering and raking in the dough. It didn't appear to be much, given the chips on the table, but she was happy nonetheless. He didn't realize the woman was with Alex Drakos until he saw Alex place his arm around her waist. For some reason, it surprised Reno. She didn't seem like Alex's type. Especially when Reno considered that Alex had wanted to fuck his wife, a woman Reno considered to be at the top of the food chain when it came to desirable women.

But he also knew people's taste could change. Maybe after the death of his son, Alex was turning over a new leaf. Getting his act together. Or maybe he was still old Alex, fucking anything he could get his hands on. But whatever.

"There's the man," Reno said as he approached.

When Alex and Kari turned toward the sound, Alex smiled too. "Well if it's not Reno Gabrini. My competitor."

"Competitor my ass," Reno responded jokingly. "You just got in the game. I changed the game. You'd better get a life, motherfucker!"

Both men laughed, and Reno extended his hand. "How are you, Alexander?"

"I'm great," Alex responded, as they shook hands. "How are you?"

"On the verge of a nervous breakdown," Reno said, rifling through his already ruffled hair. "About to put a bullet through my brain if these fuckers don't leave me alone. But other than that? I'm good."

Although Both men laughed, Kari was shocked by the bombastic style of the man before them. Was this really the owner of the PaLargio? He was, because Alex called him by his name. But she was expecting some button-down stuff shirt with his nose all in the air. But this guy, with his wrinkled-looking suit, and his unshaven face, and his bloodshot blue eyes, looked more like a gambler with a gambling problem, than the owner of the place.

Since Kari was staring at him, Reno looked at her. "And who, may I ask, is this?" he asked. "Or are you two not together?"

"We're together," Alex quickly said, and placed his hand around Kari's waist. "Reno, I want you to meet my lady--"

Reno interrupted him before he could continue. "Your lady? So you've got a lady now?"

"That's right."

Reno seemed surprised. Kari didn't understand why. She knew she shouldn't ask. This man would probably think she was so out of their league if she did ask. But since she already knew she wasn't in their league, and that reality was no big deal to her, she asked anyway. "You seem surprised," she said to Reno.

At first, she could see a little bit of that *who the fuck are you to ask me a question* look in his eyes. But then he nodded. "I am," he said. "Matter of fact."

Alex, who saw that momentary look in Reno's eyes, too, rescued his lady and took over her questioning. "Why would you be surprised?" he asked Reno.

"Why do you think? The times I've seen you around Vegas and you had some chick on your arm, you never introduced her as your lady. Not one time. Meaning no disrespect, young lady," he added, looking at Kari, "but I'm just going to tell it like it is. Those females were just sex kittens to this guy. They were no big deal." Then he looked at Alex again. "But now, all of a sudden, you want to introduce this one as your lady? I'd say I'm surprised. You've elevated this one."

Kari was a little shocked by how real he kept it, but Alex didn't seem to be.

"She's definitely not one of them," Alex responded to Reno.

Reno smiled. "Well good. About time your horny ass settled down."

Alex smiled, too. "Who's settling down? I'm amped up, if anything."

Reno laughed.

"But this is my lady, I'm very proud to say," Alex said, continuing the introduction. "This is Kari Grant."

Reno smiled. "Nice to meet you," he said as they shook hands. "Any kin to that other Cary Grant? And I know, it's a stupid question since you have the exact same name, right?

Kari smiled. "I'm used to the question. But my Christian name is actually Karena. Everybody just calls me Kari, and not with a C and a Y, but with a K and an I. So no, I'm no kin to the actor."

Reno smiled and nodded. "Well good to meet you, Kari. You seem like a very nice person. Well-spoken. Intelligent. Got it together in every way. But that only begs the question."

Kari and Alex were both confused. "What question is that?" Kari asked.

"Why the hell are you with this loser?" Reno asked, motioning his head toward Alex. "You can do better than him!"

Alex laughed. Kari smiled, but then she responded. "Actually," she said, "I don't think I can. I don't think anyone can."

Alex and Reno said "*Ooooh!*" at the same time, as if they both understood that Kari had held her own against Reno's put down of her man. Then Alex happily turned to Kari and he and she high-fived.

"What do you say about that, old man?" Alex, grinning, asked Reno.

But Reno was staring at Kari. He was impressed by her refusal to even joke about Alex. "I'd say you'd better hold on tight to that one," he said.

Alex's smile slowly dissolved, and he and Reno exchanged a glance. And Alex nodded. "I think you're right," he said.

But Reno, a man who prided himself on getting quick reads on people, suddenly saw that side of Kari that made him understand Alex's attraction to her. It wasn't about her looks, which were just okay in the full scheme of things, but it was about her guts. She had guts. It reminded him of his own wife.

But like Trina when she and Reno first met, Reno wondered if this one really understood what she was getting herself into? Did she know about the real Alex Drakos? It took Reno time and a lot of private investigators sent to Greece to find out himself. Did she want to hitch her wagon to a man with that kind of background? To a man with the kind of nasty life Reno himself knew all too well?

And suddenly Reno's protective side overtook him, and he felt a need to warn her. He looked at Kari. "He's no angel," he said to her.

"Neither am I," she said to him.

Alex again laughed and shook his head. To not just have found a good woman, but one who wasn't too timid to stand up to Reno Gabrini, was a sight to behold. He was loving it!

But Alex was cautious, too. He didn't know Gabrini well, but he'd heard he could be vindictive as hell. Get the upper hand on him, and he'd cut you down to size. And although Reno was smiling, too, Alex could see more at work in his big, blue eyes.

Alex decided, once again, to run interference. "Where's Trina?" he asked.

Although Alex had his own motive for asking that question, Kari didn't know his motivation. But she did know that a sense of pain coursed through her body when he asked it. She was not looking forward to meeting this special lady as it was! She knew this Trina Gabrini had to be a serious piece of work to command the interest of these two titans.

"She's meeting us at the restaurant," said Reno casually. Kari wondered if he even knew about the attraction Alex had had to his wife. "You know how hard she works. But she promised to be there."

"Good," Alex said.

Then Reno asked if they were ready to go. They said that they were.

And they were off.

CHAPTER FIFTEEN

They rode in the limousine across town and were seated in the VIP section of the exclusive restaurant. Trina Gabrini, to Kari's disappointment, had not arrived yet, but that didn't seem to bother the men. Busy people were busy, and they were probably accustomed to waiting. Kari was, too, but she wanted to meet this lady that caught Alex attention to such a degree that he had to warn Kari about it, and get it over with.

But as the drinks were served at their table, and as Alex and Reno engaged in small-talk about golf (Reno hated it), and business, Kari also noticed that Reno Gabrini kept taking peeps at her. It was as if he was trying to figure out what Alex might have saw in her. It was a little disconcerting to have the man Alex said was known as the most powerful man in Vegas sit across from you staring at you. Kari wasn't used to that.

But Alex, without even realizing it this time, came to her rescue again when the conversation shifted from general talk to specifics. Alex asked if Reno had made a decision about joining his Apple Valley board of directors.

Reno leaned back at their table and folded his arms. He placed the back of his hand on his cheek and began rubbing the stubble on his unshaven face. Then he spoke up. "That's problematic," he said.

Alex didn't seem bothered by that response, it seemed to Kari, as he leaned back too. "In what way?" he asked.

"In every way. It'll be like a major-leaguer joining the minors."

Kari was stunned by that reference. Was he calling Alex Drakos, the head of Drakos Capital, small potatoes?

Alex had the very same question, but he grinned while asking it. "Are you calling me a minor-leaguer?" he asked Reno.

"You? Hell no," Reno responded. "I'm not calling you a minor-leaguer. Your business empire is bigger than mine, you think I don't realize who you are? But this is your first time getting into the casino business. I've been king of casinos since I was eighteen years old. Your ass just got here. What the fuck I look like joining your board?"

Kari thought Gabrini was excessively blunt, but Alex seemed to appreciate his forthrightness. She could tell, just by their body language alone, that they were two men who, begrudgingly perhaps, respected each other.

And what Kari liked about Gabrini was that he came hard, but he didn't stay there. He had an addendum to his outright rejection of Alex's offer. "But if it's my expertise you need," Reno said to Alex, "then we can talk."

Alex smiled and extended his hand. It was exactly what he was after. That board offer was just to get the conversation started. "Your expertise," Alex said happily, "will be greatly appreciated." And the two men shook hands.

"You know how this joker and I met?" Reno asked this of Kari before he released Alex's hand.

Since Kari didn't know, she shook her head. "No," she said.

"We met because his horny ass had the hots for my wife," Reno said bluntly. Then he released Alex's hand. "I thought his ass had kidnapped her."

Alex continued to smile, but he could tell Reno still harbored resentment over that incident. But it was the kidnapping part that concerned Kari. "You thought he kidnapped her?" she asked.

"I thought so, yeah. It was fucking crazy!"

"But, of course," Alex chimed in, "it was no kidnapping at all. She went with me willingly."

Reno looked at Alex with what Kari could only describe as a sharp look. Now both men were staring at each other, as if it was some kind of test of wills. This was turning out to be a tough day. It was too much testosterone for Kari!

Not that it was new to her. She was used to guys duking it out all the time. Vito used to duke it out with the best of them. But she wasn't used to this gentlemanly way of getting that upper hand. It was too taxing on the mind and spirit all at once. Especially since it involved another woman. She thought about excusing herself to the restroom, just to get away from it all. But just as she was about to do so, the star of the show arrived.

Both men rose to their feet when Trina Gabrini arrived, and Kari was happy that she had a ringside seat and could size her up before she made it to their table. And what she saw was impressive. Like Kari, Trina was African-American, too. She had a fast gait, a curvaceous figure, and a look about her that made it clear she was the boss. Even a bombastic drama king like Reno Gabrini, it seemed to Kari, was more than happy to turn the stage over to that one.

Reno, in fact, was smiling when he first saw his wife, but when she approached, his words didn't seem to match his eyes. "About time your ass made it," he said, which surprised Kari in its harshness.

"Fuck you, Reno," Trina responded, which surprised Kari even more. These two, she thought, fought dirty. But then they gave each other a very passionate kiss, and smiled the warmest smile at each other. They might have fought dirty, Kari decided, but they probably loved dirty too.

But then Trina looked at Alex and Kari. "Sorry I'm late, guys. Hey, Alex," she added with a smile, as she sat beside her husband.

"Good to see you again," Alex said as he sat down. "I want you to meet somebody."

Trina smiled and looked at Kari. "You must be the great Kari Grant," she said.

Kari was surprised that she knew her name. Especially since her husband had known nothing about her. "I don't know about the great part," she said, "but I'm Kari"

Trina laughed. "Oh, don't sell yourself short. Alex certainly hasn't. We've only spoken a couple of times since he met you, but he spoke very highly of you both times."

"And I still didn't do her justice," Alex said.

"See," Trina said with a smile. "Alex thinks you're great."

Kari smiled.

"He offered my wife a job in his conglomerate," Reno said to Kari. "I don't know if he mentioned it to you."

"He did, yes," Kari responded.

Reno was pleased to know it. At least Drakos wasn't keeping that much from her.

"That's why we were communicating," Trina pointed out, as she took a sip of the drink her husband had already ordered for her. "I had questions about his offer, and would ask how he was doing just to get the conversation going. But then he'd launch into this long discussion, not about his job offer, but about you."

Kari laughed.

"He really likes you," Trina said. "And that's saying a lot for Alexander Drakos."

"Now that's the truth," Reno agreed.

"I would say," Alex said, disagreeing with them, "that it says more about who Kari is, and what she's made of."

Kari's heart melted inside. She'd never, not ever, met a man who treated her in public with the same level of affection he treated her in private. No matter where they went; no matter who they were around, Alex made it his business to put her on a pedestal. She was so not used to this. It made her feel so special that it scared her.

She had been so worried about this meeting, and how he would treat her when Mrs. Gabrini showed up. She was worried that he would ignore her or treat her rudely, and elevate Mrs. Gabrini to prove that he was still available if she wanted him. But just the reverse happened. He elevated Kari the way he always did, Trina or no Trina, and even the Gabrinis seemed impressed.

But Kari was also a realist. She also knew Alex could be elevating her this way to get back at Trina for her earlier rejection of his advances, and Kari was just a pawn in his more elaborate scheme. She didn't know Alex well enough to say whether or not he had that in him, but she would be shocked beyond words if he did.

And after dinner, when Kari and Trina excused themselves to the ladies' room, Trina made a pronouncement.

They were both at the vanity mirror, freshening their makeup, when Trina stopped and looked at Kari. "I'm going to turn down Alex's offer," she said.

Kari didn't stop putting on her lipstick, but she did look at Trina through the mirror. "Are you?"

"I've decided to, yes."

"He's going to be very disappointed. He believes you will make a great CEO for his startup."

"I know. And I'm honored, believe me. We, as black women, don't get that kind of offer every day."

"Word," Kari agreed.

"But I have to refuse it."

A thought suddenly occurred to Kari as she closed her lipstick tube. She looked at Trina. "I hope it's not because of his attraction to you," she said.

Trina looked at her. She wasn't sure that he had even mentioned that to Kari. But she was glad he had. She liked Kari. She couldn't put her finger on why, but she had a sneaking suspicion that, someday, they were going to be good friends. "From my perspective, no," she said. "Alex is so over me it's not even funny."

Kari grinned. "I wouldn't go that far!"

"I would!" Trina said with a smile of her own. Then she leaned against the vanity. "But from my husband's perspective," she continued, "it's a definite no-go."

"He's opposed?"

"He says he's not. He says he wants what's best for me and turning down such a generous offer could be tough. But if I know anybody on the face of this earth, I know Dominic "Reno" Gabrini. And I know that man will not want me around anybody who once harbored those kinds of feelings for me. For his sake, I'm turning it down."

Kari appreciated her loyalty to her husband. But . . . "You said it yourself. Black women don't get these kind of offers every day."

"I know. But a woman doesn't get a man like Reno every day, either. I'd rather keep Reno."

Kari smiled. She already felt that way about Alex, too, but wasn't ready to reveal that publicly yet. Even though, she had to admit, she really did like Trina Gabrini.

CHAPTER SIXTEEN

After dinner, Reno decided to ride with his wife back to the PaLargio, where Alex and Kari planned to stay the night, rather than in the limo that had brought them to the restaurant.

Alex slouched down in the backseat of the limo, while Kari answered a text message from Jordan, as the limo took off. Reno, being Reno, got behind the wheel of his wife's car and flew off. A drama king behind the wheel of a car, too, Kari thought.

Alex smiled. Reno was one of a kind, to be sure. "He seemed happy when Trina turned me down," Alex said to Kari as their limo pulled off far slower, and obeyed the speed limits heading back.

"He certainly appeared happy," Kari responded. When she finished answering Jordan's text, she looked at him. "But are you okay with her decision not to take the job?"

"I'm actually relieved," he said.

Kari was surprised to hear that. "Relieved? Why would you be relieved?"

"When I offered it to her, I cannot lie. I had honorable intentions for offering her that job. I believed she would make an excellent CEO. But I had nefarious intentions as well."

"Nefarious in what way?" Kari asked.

Alex was blunt. "I wanted to fuck her," he said.

Kari wasn't shocked at all. It was what it was.

"But now," Alex continued, "after meeting you, it's different."

"Different how?" Kari asked.

"When I look at her now, I don't want her like that. I honestly don't." He looked at Kari. "I want you like that."

Kari looked at him. "But that should be all the more reason you want to hire her," she said. "You can handle it."

"But out of respect for you," Alex said, "I don't want to have to handle it."

Kari smiled. And leaned against him.

But as they continued to drive in silence, Alex began what he called his eye sweep. He looked around, to make sure everything was Copa static. From what he could see, it all was.

Until he looked again, which was his way. He noticed something so slight he doubted if anybody else would have even thought to view it as different. But he had completed an eye sweep when they first got into the limousine to drive over to the restaurant. The man who had driven them to the restaurant wore a chauffeur's hat, too, but his hair was a darker brown, and it hung just below the nape of his neck. Unless the driver went to the hairdresser's while they were eating and got a cut and color, this driver had shorter hair with a lighter, reddish tint. Which meant, in Alex's world, he was not the same driver.

Alex remained slouched down, but he calmly pulled out his loaded revolver. Kari saw it, and her heart skipped a beat when she saw it, but she was not about to give it away. As their eyes met, she decided to just talk.

And she talked about Jordan and how he was texting her about the fun he was having with his godparents. Alex, glad that she instinctively knew how to play this, kept his eyes on the driver. He also placed a silencer on his revolver, as a just in case.

And as soon as the chauffeur turned down a side street, and Alex saw a car waiting at the end of the street, he knew shit was going down.

Knowing the limo was completely tinted, Alex wasted no time. He immediately pointed the gun at the driver's head. "Put the car in Park," Alex ordered, "or you're dead."

The chauffeur quickly stopped the limo and placed it in Park.

"Now get your ass in the passenger seat," Alex ordered.

The chauffeur quickly raised his hands as he got over into the passenger seat.

Alex quickly got behind the wheel and continued to drive. He didn't want to give whomever was in that waiting car a chance to know something was wrong.

"How many?" he asked the driver, with his gun still pointed at him.

"Four," the driver responded.

"Put your hat on my head," Alex ordered, and the man did as he was told.

Alex didn't have time to ask any more questions. He shot the driver through the head, causing blood to splatter on the passenger side window, and the chauffeur's lifeless body to slump against the passenger door. It also caused Kari to flinch and almost lose control and scream, it was so sudden.

But Alex didn't wait for her shock to ease. "Get his gun," he ordered her.

Kari knew that four men were waiting to ambush them, so she quickly did as she was told. She moved closer to the front seat, and took the chauffeur's gun from out of his pocket.

"Use it," Alex ordered.

"I will," said Kari. She'd held a gun before when she was fooling with Vito's crazy butt. Shot one before too. But this felt far more dangerous.

And as soon as the limo, driven by Alex, approached the waiting vehicle, four armed men got out of the car. But Alex was ready for their asses. He rolled down his window and Kari's window, who sat just behind him, and swerved the limo away from the car. Then he began shooting and took out numbers one and two before they could raise their weapons, while Kari quickly took out number three. Number four, however, got off some rounds.

"Get down, Kari!" Alex yelled at her. "Get your ass down!"

Kari dropped down as Alex sped away from the incoming fire. The gunman got into the middle of the street and fired round after round after round after round. He aimed to kill and was firing and firing.

Until he was firing, and no more bullets came out.

As the man quickly tossed aside the empty gun and ran to grab a gun off of one of his fallen colleagues, so that he could fire more rounds, Alex hit on brakes, got out of the limo, and it was his turn to walk toward the gunman firing round after round toward his ass. Alex shot the gunman repeatedly, until he, like his comrades, was dead in the street too.

Then Alex went around to the front passenger side of the limo, pulled the chauffeur out and tossed him onto the street, too, and then closed the door, ran around, and got back into the limo. He was looking around for more action. But none came.

But he took no chances. He got back behind that wheel and sped off. "Are you okay?" he was asking Kari, and looking through the rearview at her, as he drove.

"I'm good," she said, sitting up. "I'm good."

"Come up here," he ordered, and she did as she was told.

Alex, to her surprise, pulled her into his arm as he drove. He was breathing heavily.

"Where was security?" Kari asked him. She was breathing heavily too.

"I didn't think I needed any," Alex responded.

Kari was surprised to hear it, since he kept security on her in Apple Valley at all times. But she didn't say anything. She knew he was already upset with himself.

But Alex was more than upset. He was disgusted with himself. And that disgust, and anger he felt toward himself for being so shortsighted when he knew Kari would be with him in Vegas, was palpable.

He held her tighter.

CHAPTER SEVENTEEN

The Presidential suite was second only to Reno and Trina's luxurious penthouse apartment at the PaLargio, and Alex and Kari were the guests of honor inside that suite. But what was to be a wonderful day in Vegas, and a wonderful night in that very suite, turned out to be a nightmare.

Alex had been on the phone since they returned from the crime scene, as he paced the floor ordering his security team to get a detail to Vegas, and to find out everything they could about that planned attack. He was also calling contacts he knew in the underworld, to find out if they'd heard anything too. But so far, he was turning up blanks.

Kari was on the sofa, with Trina sitting beside her with her arm around her. Trina knew exactly how she felt. She'd been in so many ambushes with Reno, and the kind of close calls that still gave her chills, that she could write a book. But right now, she just wanted to make sure Kari was okay.

"I'm okay," Kari said to Trina for what felt like the tenth time. "I'm still a little antsy, that's all."

"I'm sorry you had to go through it," Trina said. "Especially with Alex. I never knew he . . ."

"Had that kind of background?" Kari asked her.

Trina nodded. "Yeah. He's a businessman. That's all I knew him to be. I mean, I heard that his family in Greece might have some dealings, but I never thought he had that in him too. That he was one of *them*."

"He's not," Kari said. Alex had told her that he had been very much involved in his family's business back in Greece, but that he gave it all up after he relocated to the States. She assumed, at the time, that he had told her that very personal info in confidence. And although she liked Trina very much, and was looking forward to getting to know her better, she wasn't going to go into details about what she'd been told.

But Trina shared with her, and in that moment changed their relationship.

"I hear what you're saying," Trina said. "You're saying he's not involved in his family business, but he is involved in it too. I know how it goes. It's just like my husband. His father's enemies became his enemies. His father's business became his burden. And is to this day. Trust me, I know."

Kari was shocked. Was Reno Gabrini, the owner of the famed PaLargio Hotel and Casino, connected to the mob? Was that what she was telling her?

Trina smiled when she saw Kari's reaction. "You didn't know," she said. "Didn't you?"

Kari shook her head. "No, I didn't."

"Not even a quick Google search?" Trina asked.

"Not even that. I didn't think there would be anything to find out. He owned the PaLargio. That, I thought, spoke for itself."

Trina nodded. "And for the most part, it does. But people have pasts. Sometimes we can live them down, like you and me. Sometimes we can't, like my husband and your man."

Then the door to the suite was opened, and Reno walked in.

"Speaking of the devil," Trina said with a smile.

"I love your ass too," Reno responded.

"I'll call you back," Alex said to the person on the phone, and ended the call. He looked at Reno. "Found out anything?" he asked.

"This is my town," Reno said. "It happened in my town. What do you think? Have a seat," he said, as Alex sat in the chair. Reno took the seat beside Kari and his wife.

"What did you find out?" Alex asked.

"First of all," Reno said, "where the fuck is your security?"

Kari looked at Alex. She knew how badly he already felt about that oversight. Alex crossed his legs.

"I mean, come on now," Reno continued. "You can't make that kind of mistake. Not when you've got a woman now. Not when you just lived through that ambush in Florida."

Kari was shocked. "An ambush?" she asked. "There was another attack, Alex?"

Alex had no intention of Kari ever finding out. But that cat was loose now. "Yes," he said.

"Why didn't you tell me?"

"There was nothing to tell," Alex said. "I defused the situation."

"Like hell you did," Reno said. "You took out Vito Visconni--"

Kari was surprised. "Vito?" she asked.

Now Trina was surprised. "You know this Vito person?"

"Yes. I used to live with him. What about Vito?" she asked Alex.

"He's the one I was told had hired guys to ambush me. And I had to take care of that."

Kari fully understood. They could have taken Vito out even before then, but he was suffering and they decided to let him suffer. He was begging to die then. He didn't give a damn about getting revenge. He just wanted to die. What changed?

"After you took care of that," Reno said, "my sources are telling me that his uncle didn't take too kindly to the way you took care of that."

"His uncle?" Kari asked. "What uncle?"

"His uncle," Reno said. "Wise guys have uncles. Some are related to them by blood. Some are related to them by other means. His uncle."

"Did your sources say where this uncle could be located?" Alex asked.

"Yes," Reno said.

As soon as Reno spoke that word, Alex rose to his feet.

"Alex?" Kari said, rising too. This prompted Trina and Reno to stand as well.

"Where is he?" Alex asked.

"I'll tell you where," Reno said, "if I go with you."

"No," Alex said. "I work alone. Where is he?"

Reno stared at Alex. A man had to do what a man had to do. "You'll need more firepower than I'm sure your ass brought with you."

"I might have left security at home," Alex said, "but I didn't leave my protection. Give me the address, and I'll take it from there."

"There's no address. This crazy fuck lives in the woods. But I can draw you a map."

"That'll work," Alex said, and Reno went over to the bar counter with pad and pen.

But Alex looked at Kari. His eyes, she thought, were hard and soft at the same time. It was as if he was telling her, with those eyes, that everything would be alright, but only if he made it so. And then he followed Reno.

Trina looked at Kari. She knew what it felt like to stay back while your man went away to war, as it were. But when Kari returned her gaze, and Trina could see the unshed tears in her bright, brown eyes, she put her arm around her.

"He's beating himself up enough over this," Kari said in a voice Alex nor Reno could hear. "I don't want him to see me this way."

Trina's heart went out to her. She was falling hard for Alex. "Come on," Trina said, took the younger woman in her arms, and escorted her toward the balcony.

But when Alex saw them heading that way, he stopped them. "Kari?" he asked. "Where are you going?"

"She's okay," Trina said. "We're just getting some air."

"Is it safe?" Alex asked anxiously.

"Is it safe?" Reno asked.

"This is the PaLargio, Alex," Trina said. "Reno runs this place like it's Fort Knox. There's no sharpshooters waiting to mow us down this high up. Trust, okay?"

Alex exhaled. He wanted to make eye contact with Kari, but Trina had her well buried within her bosom like some mother hen. Since he knew Kari undoubtedly needed that comfort, especially from somebody like Trina who understood turmoil, he didn't interfere. And Trina and Kari went outside.

Once outside, Trina sat Kari on the leather couch away from the sliding glass door and Alex's view, and sat down beside her. She kept her arm around her. And it was only then did Kari shed a tear.

"I'm sorry," Kari said. "But it can be difficult sometimes."

"I know," Trina said, wiping Kari's tear away. "You think you've met the man of your dreams, only to find out he comes with an occasional nightmare too."

"But Alex is wonderful. I've never met a man like him. And the way he treats me, oh, Trina. It's far and above the way anybody's ever treated me."

"But?"

"But that occasional nightmare you mentioned," Kari said, "is because of me. It's my ex-boyfriend that caused all of this. It's my poor choices that led him to have to risk his life over and over. He's no gangster. He was out of that life. But I--"

"But you nothing, Kari," Trina said firmly. "And don't think for a second the gangster life is something you can put down like a bad suit and never have to pick up again. Truth is, he's going to always have to pick it up. Tonight, it might be because of your ex. Tomorrow night, it might be because of his ex. The night after that, it could be because of some enemy he doesn't even remember. Whatever the reason, it's all the same. And trust me, nine times out of ten, it's going to be about him and his past, not you and yours."

Kari understood what Trina was saying, but still! "I should be used to upheaval," Kari said. "I've been around crooks and gangsters all my life. Beginning with my own father. But this is on a different level, Trina. That was child's play compared to this."

Trina smiled. She remembered feeling that same way early in her relationship with Reno. "And that will always be nothing but the truth," she said. "But what it means is that there's only two questions to answer."

Kari looked at the older woman. "What?" she asked.

"Is he worth it, number one," Trina said. "And are you worth it, number two."

"Yes, he's worth it," Kari could easily answer. "Am I worth it? You mean to him?"

"Are you going to be able to handle the hell days, that's what I mean," Trina said. "Do you have what it takes? When the shit hits the fan, and it's fight or flight, are you going to stay and fight, or turn tail and run? Are you up for the danger, the challenge, and the monumental rewards? That's what I mean."

Kari thought about it, but it really wasn't close. "If it means I'll have Alex?" she asked. "Hell yeah!"

Trina smiled, and then laughed, and then hugged Kari vigorously. "I knew you was down," she said. "No shade, but I knew it when I first saw you! I said to myself, now this sister right here got game. Oh, yeah, she's been around that block a time or two. Just like me. Ain't no shrinking violet nowhere in her!"

Kari smiled too, and despite the craziness she'd just endured, and the craziness Alex had yet to endure, she couldn't help but laugh.

CHAPTER EIGHTEEN

Alex parked on the side of the dirt road that led to the pathway. There was one way in and one way out, according to Reno, but Alex found another way. He walked, fully armed, through thickets of trees and branches for half a mile away from the entrance.

When he saw the small cabin in those woods, he stopped walking to make sure there was no one on his tail, or positioned around the place. All he heard were the night cries of the night insects. But no human sounds. He proceeded forward.

After carefully walking around the cabin, checking out the front door and the back door, he decided the back door was more vulnerable. He therefore walked back around to the front of the cabin, banged vigorously on the front door, and then ran to the back of the cabin.

After several seconds, the front door was flung open by a man known around those parts as Snipe, and he opened that door with a sawed-off shotgun locked and loaded. "Who's the motherfucker banging on my door like that?" he yelled as soon as he opened up.

But while Snipe was distracted at the front door, Alex kicked in the backdoor, and entered in the house with his own rifle aimed and ready.

It was what they called a shotgun house, and Snipe turned around quickly to the sound. But Alex was running toward him as soon as he turned. Snipe fired a shot as soon as he saw the intruder, but Alex had already launched his body at him, knocking him down and causing him to fire erratically. Alex knocked Snipe's gun, along with Snipe, to the floor.

But when Snipe realized who it was that had tackled him down, he jumped back up and attempted to run away.

He made it to the back bedroom with Alex close on his trail. But just as he was slamming the door in an attempt to lock it, Alex's big body shouldered it back open, splintering it so violently that wood chips flew around the room like confetti.

Snipe backed up, looking around for something to grab in his defense, but Alex grabbed him, lifted his entire body up, and angrily threw him out of an unopened window, shattering the glass.

As Snipe lay on the ground outside, in severe pain from the glass breaking around him and the fall itself, Alex jumped out of that window, too, and made his way to Snipe's side.

He grabbed Snipe by the shirt until Snipe was sitting up. Cuts were all over his face and neck. "Why?" Alex asked him. "Because I crippled your sorry-ass nephew? Because I killed his ass?"

But Snipe wouldn't answer him.

Alex punched him mercilessly in the face. "Why, motherfucker? Are you the one who sent those goons to Florida to try that shit there too? Was it you all along, and not Vito?"

When Snipe didn't respond, and Alex was about to rough him up some more, he gave in. "Yes," Snipe finally said, and he said it defeatedly. "It was me."

Alex stared at him, sizing him up. "Lying motherfucker," he said.

Snipe looked at him.

"I researched your ass before I came here," Alex said. "You're the one who killed Vito's old man, which happens to be your own brother. You killed your own brother and did time in prison for it, too. So I figure a man like that, why would he give a fuck about Vito? He was a nephew to you in name only anyway."

Alex pulled him closer, but this time he pulled out his handgun and placed it to Snipe's head. "Now you tell me the truth, motherfucker," he said, "or when I leave, I'm taking your head with me. Are you going to tell me the truth?"

Snipe quickly nodded that he would. Alex just as quickly removed the gun from his head. "Now talk," he said. "Who hired you to handle that Florida hit, because I know your ass didn't come up with that shit all by yourself? Who hired you to pull off that shit y'all pulled tonight?"

Snipe began shaking his head.

Alex grabbed him again, ready to put that gun back to his head.

"Your brother," Snipe blurted out.

Alex stared at him. "What?"

"Your brother hired me."

Alex fired. "My brother?"

"Since I did to my own brother what he wants to do to you, he figured I would make the perfect person to pull it off. I'm experienced at this shit. And I would have done it, too. But I hired out. I figure why get my hands dirty? That fucker paid me in advance, anyway. And the guys I hired weren't the best, but I figured it wasn't that hard a job. You were just a rich business man, what could you do? But you took them out in Florida, and when I hired a second crew to do the job in Vegas, you took them out too."

Snipe shook his head as if he was mighty regretful. "They failed," he said. "Every one of those fuckers I hired failed. But I won't!" Snipe said suddenly and grabbed Alex's gun in a desperate attempt to wrestle it away from him.

Snipe was strong. He had prison yard muscles and he and Alex tussled mightily for control of that weapon. But he was not strong enough to overpower Alex Drakos. Alex took control of his own weapon, turned it toward Snipe's terrified face, and fired.

But when Alex made the run back to his vehicle, and then sped away from the scene, he was still reeling from the news. He called Jimmy Hines, his conglomerate's chief investigator.

"Get to Greece, Jim," he ordered. "I was just told that Odysseus ordered a hit on me. I was just told that my own brother wants me dead. Find out if it's true."

"Yes, sir," the chief said, his voice as stunned as Alex's.

And when Alex made it back to the Presidential suite at the PaLargio, Alex was impressed with the level of security around the place. His men had arrived, but Reno had men in place, too.

Inside the suite, Reno and Trina had gone, and Kari was sitting up in bed asleep, with a book called *The Unauthorized Biography of the Billionaire Playboy*, a biography on Alex's life, sitting on her lap.

Alex, with his hands in his pockets and his brows knitted, stood at the bedside and stared at her. If they stayed together, he thought, she would have no idea what she was getting herself into. He had thought he could keep it separately. Other than this drama with Vito Visconni, there had been no issues. But suddenly there were plenty of issues, and not least of which might just involve his own brother. If it turned out to be true, he knew keeping it from her would be an impossibility. And he was so damned attached to her already. Could he let her go, to save her?

But just as that thought entered his mind, Kari's eyes opened. And when she saw Alex standing there, in one piece, a brilliant smile came over her face. And she tossed the book aside, jumped from the bed, and fell into his arms.

"Oh, Alex, you're safe!" she cried as she held him. "You're safe!"

He might have been safe tonight, he thought, but that wasn't the question. Was she going to be safe, he thought, was the question.

CHAPTER NINETEEN

Monday morning and Kari had picked up Jordan from Faye and Benny's, and was driving him to school. He had stayed at their place Sunday night, too, because they had attended a concert at church that didn't end until very late, and since Kari had not yet made it back in town, he opted to stay the night there. But now Alex was back in New York, Kari was back in Apple Valley, and life was trying to get back to normal. If there was any such thing anymore.

And Jordan, her usually chipper son, seemed down in the dumps. "You didn't tell me how you enjoyed your weekend," she said.

"It was okay," Jordan said as joyless as he could possibly have said it.

"You went to church last night?"

"And that morning and afternoon too. Is there ever a Sunday when Auntie Faye and Uncle Benny don't go to church?"

"What was the sermon about?" Kari asked.

"Treating people right," Jordan said, and then he looked at his mother. "How did he treat you?"

Kari knew exactly who the *he* was. "What kind of question is that?"

"How did he treat you, Ma? Did he treat you right?"

"Yes. Of course he did! He always does. Why would you ask something like that?"

"Did he ask you to marry him?" Jordan asked.

Kari frowned. "Marry him? Jordan, what are you talking about? We're still trying to get to know each other. What's wrong with you, boy?"

She glanced at him as she drove. Not enough to get a good read on what he might have been thinking, but enough to tell he was upset about something. "What is it, J?" she asked him.

Jordan exhaled. "I saw something online," he said.

"About what?" she asked.

"About Alex." Jordan looked at his mother. "And his fiancée."

Kari's heartbeat began to quicken. "Don't you believe everything you read online. There's nothing but lies on the internet."

At first, there was silence. Then she couldn't help herself. "What did you read?" she asked.

"I heard he bought this big diamond ring for Natalie Corman."

"Natalie Corman?" Kari was stunned. "The actress?"

Jordan nodded. "She says she and Alex are going to be married. Married, Ma! And she's very beautiful. I mean, she's very, very beautiful." He looked at his mother again. "How are we going to compete against that? We drive a Toyota Tercel. We live in a tiny little house. We're barely getting by!"

Kari pull up to the drop-off station at Arapaho Middle School.

"How are we going to compete against her?" Jordan asked again.

"We aren't going to compete against any one," Kari said firmly, although her heart was hammering. "We won't have to. Whatever she said just isn't true."

Jordan stared at her. "How can you say it's not true?"

"Because it's not true, Jordan, that's how. You hear me? It's not true. Alex wouldn't do that."

"You're always telling me you barely know him, you're still trying to get to know him, but yet you're going to believe that lady is lying? Why would a big-time actress like Natalie Corman lie, Ma? That's crazy. It's official, she said. I saw the ring, Ma!"

Kari could see the pain in his eyes. And she was in so much pain herself she didn't know how to comfort him. But she did know this: there was nothing neither one of them could do about it now. "Don't you worry about that at all," she said to her son. "You hear me, Jordan? Don't worry about that. You go to your classes and get your work. You do like that preacher said and treat everybody right. God's got this. We're good."

Jordan looked at his mother. She was always putting on the brave front, no matter what. But he knew she was hurting. That was why he didn't want to tell her when he first saw it on the internet late last night. But he knew if anybody was going to tell her, it was only right that it would be him.

Although it was like the most uncool thing ever to his friends at Arapaho Middle, he reached over anyway and hugged his mother. She deserved happiness more than anybody alive, if you asked Jordan, but she was always the one who never ended up with any. He gladly hugged her neck.

And Kari gladly received the hug as she fought back tears. Jordan was the only example she had in her entire life that turned out to be a home run, with no ands if or buts in the bargain. Jordan, when it came down to it, was all she had.

And when they finished hugging, she managed to smile. "If you're good," she said, "as I know you will be, I'll cook you your favorite spaghetti tonight."

Jordan tried to smile but he was too much of an emotional child. "Okay, Ma," he said, gathered up his bookbag, and got out of the car.

But as Kari drove away, she was angry.

"Damn! Damn! Damn!" she said out loud as she drove; as she gripped the steering wheel and hit her palm up against it. She didn't know if any of what that actress said was true, but that wasn't the point to her. She fell for some guy who still had mess to clean up, and now her son was in as deep as she was. Now Jordan felt as hurt as she felt. She dragged her own son into this shit when she swore she'd never do that again! That was the worst part.

But it was more than that, too. She even had Alex risking his life, over and over, because of her stupid decision when she wasn't even eighteen, and with a dead man's baby no less, to hook up with a bastard like Vito Visconni to begin with. What kind of sorry-ass, can't-do-anything-right piece of crap she really was?

But even Kari knew, as she drove further and further away, that she was only lashing out at herself because that news Jordan had just unloaded on her hurt.

Bad

CHAPTER TWENTY

Matt Scribner, the chief financial officer at Drakos Capital, thought about it. And then he thought about it some more. He was in Alex's office, seated in front of Alex's desk. His elbows rested on both arms of the chair and his fingers were tented in front of him. "I would define it more as good progress," he said, "but not great progress. We break ground in a month, that's still on track as of today. But we still have a ton of cost overrun inclusions that are receiving push back after push back. Every one of the companies are demanding more incentives as a part of the package. They all feel our agreements are too punishment-heavy against them."

"Damn right they're punishment heavy against them," Alex responded. He sat behind his desk. "What do they expect? For it to be punishment-heavy against *me*? They fought tooth-and-nail to be a part of this project, because they all know what it'll mean for their bottom lines. The cards are in my hands. Not theirs. What did they think I was going to do?

They thought I would deal myself a bad hand, and deal them a better one?"

"According to them, not that I agree with it, but according to them they want the deck stacked with a little more balance in mind."

Alex shook his head. "They want me to balance the deck against myself when every one of those greedy bastards know I can turn down their demands and hire brand new contractors as easily as I hired them. No. No deal. You tell them the contracts remain as written. If they want to bow out, they have until close-of-business Friday of this week. They can bow out up until then without penalty. But no more negotiations. That's over."

"We're playing hardball then?" the CFO asked.

"As hard as we can throw it," Alex said. "I committed to the citizens of Apple Valley that I would have this project on time and under budget, and that's exactly what is going to happen."

Alex's desk intercom buzzed.

"Then that's what will happen," the CFO said. "I'll put the word out."

Alex pressed the intercom button. "Yes?"

"Mr. Hines is here, sir." Jimmy Hines was Alex's chief investigator.

"Send him through," Alex said and released the button. Then he looked at Scribner. "Get to it then," he said to him.

The CFO smiled as he rose to his feet. "Get lost, in other words?" he asked.

Alex smiled too. "Those would be the exact words, yes!"

The CFO laughed as he headed out of the door that Jimmy Hines was entering through. They spoke, but the chief only had eyes for Alex. He hurried and stood in front of Alex's desk. He was just back from Greece, and Alex could tell the intel wasn't good.

"What did you learn?" he asked.

"Couldn't get shit from anybody, Boss. Not even your brother's enemies. It's a closed society in the Grecian mob. You know how they are. They wouldn't even talk to me. They know I work for you, and they still wouldn't talk to me."

Alex was staring at his chief. He knew him like he knew the back of his hand. "But?" he asked.

"But something's up. Something so big it's got everybody spooked. I could feel it in the fucking air over there. I even tried to get an audience with your father, to tell him what happened and what you heard about it, but he wouldn't see me either."

That was news for sure, Alex thought. If his old man wouldn't so much as talk to a man he knew represented Alex, something was definitely up.

"I hate to say it, Boss," Jim Hines said, "but you've got to go to Greece and see what's going on for yourself. They won't talk to me, but they damn sure will talk to you."

The intercom button buzzed again. Alex, accustomed to constant interruptions, pressed it. "Yes?"

"The deputy chief is here to see the chief, sir."

Hines frowned. "Tell him to wait," he yelled at the intercom. "His ass knows I'm in a meeting with the boss!"

"He said," the voice over the intercom responded, "that it's about the boss, and the boss's woman."

Hines frowned. "The boss's woman? What the fuck is he talking about?"

But Alex kept his voice measured as he spoke into the intercom, although he was suddenly worried. "Send him through," he said.

That surprised the chief, and he looked back as his deputy quickly came into the office and made his way up to the desk.

"What's this about?" the chief asked. He knew how Alex felt about that black girl in Florida. Every one of his security chiefs knew it, and had been given their orders concerning her and her kid. If anything came up regarding either one of them, Alex had ordered, they were to get in touch with him personally. No back channels. No third-and-forth hand. He wanted to hear directly from them. That was why the deputy felt he was on solid ground by the interruption. But was it worth interrupting them, was the chief's question.

"I just received a phone call from our guys in the field in Apple Valley," he said.

"Go on," Alex said.

"There's rumors going around, sir. Very nasty rumors."

The chief frowned. "Rumors? You barged in on our meeting because of rumors?"

But Alex was far less dismissive. "What are the rumors about?" he asked.

"Natalie Corman is all over the internet, and as of right now on some television programs too, saying that you and she are engaged. She's displaying the engagement ring you allegedly gave to her as well."

The chief looked at Alex. "Engaged?" he asked him. That was news to him. But Alex didn't look at the chief. He was too busy staring at the deputy. More, he knew, was to come.

"We have every reason to believe that," the deputy said, "given how hot the story is in that town, and I mean it's hot, sir: we have every reason to believe that Miss Grant heard those rumors too. From what her office manager told us, and that woman is very concerned about Miss Grant, she probably saw Natalie Corman's announcement too."

Alex suspected that would be the other part. Natalie Corman went public. Her ass did it anyway. And now Kari knew.

Alex leaned back in his chair and clasped his fingers together. He didn't say anything, but his chief and deputy both could see that tightening of his jaw.

CHAPTER TWENTY-ONE

At a motel in Apple Valley, Kari was on her knees cleaning the toilet when she heard her best friend's voice.

"Kari? Kari? Kari Grant, where are you, girl?"

Kari wiped her forehead with the back of her rubber-gloved hand. "Back here," she said loudly. "In the bathroom."

"They told me you were over here," Faye Church began saying, but when she arrived in the doorway of the bathroom, she stopped in her tracks and frowned. "What on earth are you doing?" she asked.

Kari looked at her friend, who stood before her dressed in Prada head-to-toe, with keys in one hand and a Styrofoam cup of Starbucks coffee in the other. Then she continued scrubbing. "One of my girls called in sick," she said.

"Then make your other girls clean her rooms," Faye said.

"Nope," Kari said firmly. "This is a new contract. If we get behind like that, they may cancel us. I can't afford that. I'll clean every toilet in Apple Valley before I let that happen."

Faye shook her head. "You're better than me, girl. Cleaning toilets? I'll just have to lose this particular contract. I'm sorry."

"Sure you would, Faye," Kari said as she rose to her feet.

"I'm serious!"

"If you owned a business, and didn't have Benny as your backup, a man who happens to be a successful lawyer by the way, then you'd do whatever you had to do to stay afloat. Trust. Okay?"

Faye smiled. "I guess you're right."

"So what's up?" Kari began removing the rubber gloves and placing them in her supply cart. When Faye didn't respond, Kari glanced back at her.

"Did J tell you?" Faye asked.

Kari exhaled, turned toward Faye, and leaned against the sink vanity. "He told me."

"It's a crying shame, Kare. I'd kick his ass myself if he was here right now."

"Just because somebody said something on the internet doesn't make it true," Kari responded.

"But it's not just on the internet," Faye pointed out. "It's all over. Access Hollywood. TMZ. Even Wendy Williams mentioned it in her Hot Topics, and you know that woman's legit."

"But it's still gossip," Kari said as she stood erect and began pushing her cart toward the bathroom's exit, where Faye stood.

"Did he call you?" Faye asked, as she moved aside.

Kari didn't answer that. She already felt like crap. Here she was, cleaning toilets for a living, and some gorgeous actress was claiming to be engaged to Alex. And that actress's engagement to him seemed far more plausible and real to everybody in town than Kari's relationship to him.

As Kari (and her cart) walked out of the motel's bathroom, and was about to head for the next room to clean, Faye placed her hand on Kari's arm.

Kari looked at her hand, and then looked into Faye's eyes. When their eyes met, and

Kari could see that tears of empathy had pooled in Faye's eyes, those unshed tears Kari had been fighting all day appeared in Kari's eyes too. And the two friends embraced.

"You'll find you a good man, Kari," Faye said as she held her best friend. "You'll find somebody who deserves you."

They held onto each other for a long time, and then stopped embracing. Kari wiped away a tear. Faye still had her hands on both of Kari's arms. "You do believe that, don't you?" Faye asked her.

"Do I believe that good men are out there?" Kari asked. "Yes, I do. Do I believe I'll get one?"

Kari scrunched up her face. She dreaded even answering such a pitiful question. "I've got to get back to work," she said, just as her cell phone rang.

"Why don't you and Jordan come to dinner tonight?" Faye asked, as Kari pulled out her cell phone. "Benny and I would love to have you."

Kari looked at her Caller ID, and Faye immediately saw a change in her expression. "Who is it?" Faye asked. Then she realized who. "Is it him? Don't answer it if it is. Make that asshole sweat. Don't answer it, Kari!"

Kari loved Faye, but she wasn't trying to hear her. This was Kari's life. And her heart. And nobody, not even Faye, was going to dictate that. She answered the call. "Hello?"

"I'm coming to town tonight."

Just the sound of his voice caused Kari to close her eyes in a tight squeeze that left her filled with all kinds of emotions.

Alex continued: "I need to see you concerning a matter," he said.

It was true then, thought Kari. And there was no way around it: they needed to talk about it. "Okay," she said.

"Okay," said Alex. Then there was a longer-than-usual pause. "See you tonight," he added.

Kari didn't add anything. She ended the call.

"What did he say?" Faye asked anxiously.

"He's coming to town tonight."

"And?"

"We're going to talk."

Faye's heart dropped. She knew what that meant. She pulled Kari into her arms again.

CHAPTER TWENTY-TWO

Kari stirred her pot of pasta one more time and then walked over to the center island, picked up her cellphone, and continued to stare at the photograph in front of her. Natalie Corman. A gorgeous redhead all the men in Hollywood supposedly wanted. According to what Kari had been reading, this woman and Alex had been in what they called an on-again, off-again relationship for years. Now it was apparently on again, if all of these stories were to be believed. But Kari needed to hear it from Alex himself before she could become a true believer.

But what was bothering her even more was the why. Not the why of any relationship he might or might not have with that actress. But why would a man who had his pick of glamour girls like Natalie Corman decide to pitch his tent with a decidedly un-glamourous girl like Kari? That woman undoubtedly spent her afternoons getting manicures and pedicures. Kari spent her afternoon cleaning toilets!

But when Kari heard Jordan's bedroom door open, she immediately closed the screen she had been viewing on her phone. If Kari were perplexed by it all, Jordan was downright pissed.

He entered the kitchen, with his cellphone in hand, too, and sat at the center island.

"Hey."

"Hey."

"Finished your homework?"

"Yeah."

Kari stared at him.

"Yes, ma'am."

"Anything you needed me to help you with?"

"Why are you cooking for him?" Jordan asked.

Kari frowned. "What?"

"Why are you cooking for him after what he's done to you?"

"First of all, young man," Kari said, "I'm not cooking for him. I'm cooking for us. I promised to fix you spaghetti tonight, and that's exactly what I'm doing. And second of all, Alex is going to be a guest in my home tonight. He treated us well when we were in his house. We will return the favor. Especially you, buster. He ain't done shit to you!"

But Jordan was shaking his head. "That's not true," he said. "Anybody who hurts my mama, hurts me."

Kari stared at him.

"We come as a package deal," Jordan continued. "They get one, they get the other one. Whether they like it or not."

Kari smiled. And ruffled Jordan's soft hair. "You got that right," she said. "And don't be upset by what's going on, Jordan."

"It's not that I'm upset," Jordan said. "I'm just disappointed in Mr. Drakos. I thought he . . ."

Kari nodded. She thought so too.

"And don't worry, Ma," Jordan said, "he doesn't have to take care of you. Just wait until I get out of high school, and get out of college. I'm gonna buy you the biggest house you ever seen before, and I'm gonna buy you a car, too. And it ain't gonna be no Toyota Tercel!"

Kari laughed. "That's a reliable car, boy," she said. "Don't knock it!"

But Kari felt a great need to set Jordan straight. "I appreciate how you feel, J," she said. "But here's a novel idea. Why don't Alex take care of himself. Why don't you, when you're grown, take care of yourself. And I'll take care of myself. How's that for a deal?"

But Jordan was shaking his head. He was as stubborn as his mother. "Nope," he said. "I'm taking care of you."

Kari smiled again, but as soon as she did they both heard a car pull up on their driveway.

Jordan nervously looked at Kari. Kari went over to her pot, removed it from the burner and turned the burner off, and then wiped her hands on the apron she wore. Then she, followed by Jordan, went into the living room and looked out of the picture window.

Alex, this time, was driving a big Cadillac Escalade SUV, and was on his phone.

Jordan shook his head. "He's always on the phone," he said.

"He has an empire to run," Kari said. "It's amazing he's even bothering to come and talk to us at all."

But that didn't sit right with Jordan. He looked at his mother. "Stop making excuses for him," he said. "I don't want him to play you like that."

Kari laughed. "Play me? Boy, please! Nobody's playing me. I'm just pointing out the obvious. Don't you ever be so blinded by anger that you refuse to accept the truth. I taught you that. The man runs an empire. That's the truth. The man took time out of his busy schedule to come see us about whatever it is he's coming to see us about. That's the truth too. Regardless of how we may feel about him right now, the truth is still the truth. Got it?"

Jordan nodded his head. "Yes, ma'am," he said.

Kari smiled. She really didn't deserve this kid!

But when Alex got out of the SUV, and began heading toward the house, all smiles were gone. He was casually dressed, in slacks and a V-neck pullover knit shirt, and Kari's heart began to hammer. She cared so deeply for him!

Then the doorbell rang. Kari was about to answer it, but Jordan pulled her back. "You sit down," he said. "He doesn't need to think you're all anxious to see him again. I'll answer it."

Kari felt odd taking direction from her fourteen-year-old son, but he had a point. She went over to the sofa and sat down. Jordan went to the front door, and opened it.

Alex smiled when he saw his favorite teenager. "Hey, Jordan! How are you?" he asked.

Jordan, however, couldn't muster the same enthusiasm he usually had whenever he saw Mr. Drakos. "I'm okay," he said.

Alex felt the chill. He understood why. But that didn't mean it didn't hurt. "Good," he said.

And he walked on in.

Kari was seated on the sofa. Her hair was in a messy ponytail where some of the strands had escaped the enclosure. She wore an apron around her small waist, and a pair of jeans beneath it. And unlike all the women he'd ever dated, she was the only one who didn't go out of her way to impress him with clothes and jewelry and all manner of style and sophistication just to eat dinner at home. But it was Kari, above all those other women, who impressed him the most.

"Hello," he said to her as he walked toward her.

"Hey," she responded.

But when he leaned down, to kiss her on the lips, he fully expected her to recoil. Any other woman in her circumstance would. Besides, if Jordan was the barometer, he was certain she was the reason.

But Kari, to his inward delight, didn't recoil at all. She accepted his kiss. She, at least, was willing to give him the benefit of the doubt. And if he wanted anybody on the face of this earth to give him that benefit, it was Kari.

And when their lips met, it was Alex who closed his eyes tightly and felt that sweetness she always gave to him. The fact that she was hurting angered him. He had to make this right!

His plan was to sit beside her, and hold her, but Jordan came up while they were kissing and sat beside Kari himself. He was highly protective of his mother, especially when he felt she was vulnerable. Alex appreciated that. When he wasn't around, he knew he was going to be able to depend on Jordan. He was counting on it!

He sat in the chair that flanked the sofa, while mother and son stared at him. He got to it. "I've got to make a trip to Fiskardo," he said.

Jordan frowned. "To where?"

"His hometown," Kari said. "It's in Greece."

Jordan and Alex both looked at her.

"I read that much in that unauthorized biography," Kari said.

Alex smiled. "It was about the only thing in that entire book that lady got right," he said.

But then there was a pause. A very tense, awkward pause.

It was Kari who decided to get on with it. "Why are you here, Alex?" she asked him pointblank.

"I heard you've heard some things," he said.

"Such as?" Kari asked.

"About myself and Natalie Corman."

Kari nodded. Now they were getting down to it, she thought. "Yes. I've heard."

"So have I," said Jordan.

"I think you need to go to your room, Jordan," Alex began saying.

But Jordan looked at his mother, ready to object.

"But," Alex continued, "given that it's apparently the juicy topic of conversation all over this town, I think you need to hear this, too. Agreed?"

Jordan nodded his head. "Yeah," he said.

But Kari hit him upside his head. Jordan looked at her. "I don't care how upset you are, boy," she said firmly, "we will not do that. Not today. Not ever."

Jordan, knowing exactly what she meant even if Alex wasn't quite sure, looked at Alex. "I meant yes, sir," he said.

Alex understood. Despite her pain, Kari was teaching her son a lesson: respect his elders, even if he thought them to be a pile of shit.

Alex leaned forward, as if the closer he was to the two people who were quickly becoming the two most important people in his life, the more they would believe him. "Here's the story," he said. "I went out on two dates with Natalie Corman. The first one was at a dinner party in Manhattan. The second one was at some other public function that I can't even remember the name of or what it entailed. I slept with her both times," he said.

Kari hated that Jordan had to hear that, and she glanced at him, but Jordan didn't even seem fazed. Because he didn't care about any of that. That all happened in the past, before Alex met his mother. What Jordan wanted to know was in the here and now: the final verdict. Was Alex going to marry that woman?

"After those two initial meetings, I never called her again. Nor did I see her again."

"You didn't see her again?" Kari asked. "But all those stories are saying you and she have been in an on-again, off-again relationship for years."

"She's been in an imaginary, for publicity reasons, on-and-off relationship with me. Now she's starting it back up again."

"But why?" Kari asked, still confused. "And why is she all over television and the internet claiming that you and she are engaged? And why is she showing off this big rock you supposedly gave to her?"

"Because her career is waning again and she need some buzz to get back in the main. What better way to do that than to claim an engagement to the billionaire playboy, that nonsense title they have bestowed upon me?"

Kari was feeling hopeful again. So was Jordan. "So you're saying," Kari asked him, "that this is all a publicity stunt?"

"Pure and simple," Alex said. "A stunt orchestrated by Natalie herself. Normally, it would not faze me at all. She's not the only one who pulls that shit just to get a little buzz. I'm used to it. But I have you now, and Jordan, and the two of you to think about. Your reputations. My lawyers have contacted her lawyers to notify them of my intent to sue her for slander."

"But can you win a case like that?" Kari asked.

"It'll never go to court," Alex said. "But if she doesn't want me to get on television and tell the truth about what she's up to, she'll get on TV herself and correct the record. But trust me, if she continues to hold onto this charade, I will take her ass to court, and I will get on television myself and correct the record. But either way, that will be the end of that."

Jordan looked at Kari. And they both smiled. They believed Alex. He could be lying his head off, but it didn't feel like that to them. It felt like it felt before this Natalie Corman drama. It felt like Alex, and them, together again!

And Kari and Jordan both jumped up from the sofa and ran to Alex for a group embrace. Alex felt such relief, and such happiness, that he pulled them both into more than an embrace. It was more like a smothering bear hug. It was the affection Alex was hoping for when he first arrived. They were always so enthusiastic to see him. It warmed his heart in ways they would never know. Alex, in fact, never felt happier than when he was with them.

But although Jordan stood back up and managed to get out of the hug, Kari remained on Alex's lap.

Kari stood up, and then Alex with her. He looked at her. "Why don't we go for a little ride?" he asked. He was going to take her to his rental house and fuck her brains out. He'd do it right where they were, in Kari's bedroom: that would be the fastest way. But she didn't want that around Jordan.

"A drive would be nice," Kari said, "but I've got to finish Jordan's spaghetti first."

Jordan smiled. His mother never kicked him to the curb to be with some man! "That's right," he said. "She promised me her world-famous spaghetti tonight. Have you tried it yet, Mr. Drakos?"

"Not yet, no," Alex said. Then he smiled. "But it looks like I'm going to be trying it tonight."

Kari laughed, and headed for the kitchen.

But when Alex went to follow her, Jordan pulled him back.

"What is it, J?" Alex asked.

"Nobody's ever treated my mom like a queen," he said. "If you do that; if you treat her right, then we'll love you forever."

Alex's throat constricted. He wished to God he was worthy of this wonderful young man and his mother. And his look was as serious as if he had just landed a million-dollar deal. He extended his hand. "You have my word," he said, and he and Jordan shook on it.

When their handshake agreement was completed, Jordan grinned and rubbed his hands together. "Now for the spaghetti," he said.

"So your mom's a world class cook, is she?"

"With spaghetti she is."

"And with everything else?" Alex asked.

"She's not the world's best cook," Jordan admitted, "but she's better than nothing."

Alex laughed a hearty laugh. Jordan was as real as his mother. Then Alex placed his hand on Jordan's back, and followed him into the kitchen.

CHAPTER TWENTY-THREE

They took it slow. Kari was lying on top of him, stomach to stomach, and he was inside of her. As Kari laid her head on his chest, and closed her eyes to enjoy the sensations, not only of his dick inside of her, but his big, powerful hands all over her. Alex was rubbing her ass, and her back, and her ass all over again. He was squeezing both cheeks so hard that it made those sensations intensify. He was a master of control when he wanted to be, and Alex was in control that night.

Alex was in new territory that night as well. As he stroked inside of her, and slid along her wetness and ridges, he was becoming more rigid and thicker the deeper he penetrated. And he was feeling the heat. Not the heat of their sex. He was well familiar with that kind of heat. But the heat of being with somebody who made his heart feel lighter. Who made his shoulders slump in a relaxation that took away all the burdens he bore, even if just for that moment in time. Who made his mind wander to possibilities that just months before would have been absurd to him. He was in what he could only guess was love territory.

Alex Drakos could not admit it out loud, but he privately felt that he just might be falling in love.

He closed his eyes, enjoyed what it felt to be making love to the woman that just might be the one he never thought would ever be, and imagined the possibility. Karena "Kari" Grant. Kari Grant. Kari Drakos.

He opened his eyes, a little shaken by the thought. He knew it would certainly be a thousand steps up from Linda Drakos. He knew he would be proud to parade around a woman of her character and goodness as his woman. He knew he would be filled with that kind of joy that he always thought would elude him for life.

But what would it do for her?

How would he enhance her life?

He had baggage. So much baggage! How could he put that weight on her?

But he wanted her. How could he not? Because Alex Drakos always had a knack for getting exactly what he wanted.

Except when it came to love.

He pulled Kari tighter into his arms as his strokes began to increase. He knew he was going deeper into that web of love with every stroke he put on her, but he kept stroking anyway. The idea that some Hollywood whore like Natalie Corman would tell the world he had asked her to be his wife, would normally have been mildly amusing to Alex. The idea of that vicious lie being spread around now, hurting this woman in his arms, the woman his dick was impaled inside of, wasn't funny anymore.

He held Kari tighter and tighter, and fucked her harder and harder at just the thought of hurting her. And when she had her orgasm, and lifted her head and looked her hooded eyes into his hooded eyes as she came, his heart squeezed with the joy her eyes displayed. And he didn't even cum that night. Just seeing Kari happy, and satisfied, was all the cum he needed.

Alex Drakos was falling in love.

Later that night, as they lay arm in arm, Kari was feeling some kind of happy way too. She even began smiling.

Alex looked at her, and couldn't help but smile too. "What's so funny?" he asked.

"Nothing's funny," Kari said. "But it seems so quiet now. Every time I came over here there was always so much noise and activity and the sound of machines doing what machines do."

Alex smiled. "That's over for now." Then he thought about it. Now was as good a time as any to tell her, he decided. "I'm having a house built here in Apple Valley," he said.

Kari was surprised. She looked at him. "A house?"

Alex looked at her. "Yes."

What did that mean, Kari wondered? And being Kari, she had to ask it. "Does that mean you plan to move to Apple Valley?"

Alex exhaled. "I don't know yet," he said truthfully. "But just in case."

Kari smiled. "Just in case you may move here, you're having a house built here?"

"That's right."

Kari shook her head. "You are one odd hombre," she said.

Alex laughed.

When the laugher died down, she moved closer against him. "It'll be great if you did move here," she said. "I know two people who will be very happy."

Alex knew it too. He pulled her closer, and kissed her on her forehead.

After another pause of silence, Kari remembered what he had said. "You're going to Greece," she said.

Alex nodded. "Yes."

"When?"

"After the Meet and Greet."

Kari looked at him. "What Meet and Greet?"

Alex was surprised. "You didn't get an invite?"

"No."

"That's what happens when you leave it to politicians. I guess the mayor is inviting only those he wants to attend."

"What is it about?"

"It's meant to be for vendors who already have secured contracts with the hotel and casino I'm building. But also for vendors who want contracts. I'll be meeting and greeting both. It was supposed to happen later this week, but I had to push it up for tomorrow at noon."

"Because you were coming to town?"

"That, yes," Alex responded, "and because I need to get to Greece. Speaking of which," he added.

When he didn't say anything else, Kari looked at him. "What?" she asked.

"I want you to come with me."

Did Kari hear him right? "Come with you where?" she asked, to clarify it for herself.

"To Greece," Alex replied. "I want you to drop everything tomorrow afternoon, come with me to the Meet and Greet, and then board my plane and come with me to Greece."

Kari was stunned.

"I think you should meet my family," Alex said.

"You mean the gangsters?" Kari asked with a smile.

Alex looked at her. No smile. No sugarcoat. "Yes," he said. "That's why I'm going."

"What do you mean?"

"I heard something disturbing about my brother. I need to find out if it's true."

Kari wanted to ask what was it that was so disturbing, but she held her peace.

"Will you come?" he asked her. "Benny and Faye will see after Jordan. Dezzamaine will take care of *Maid for Mom*, I'm sure, while we're gone."

But he could tell Kari was waffling. He decided to make himself plain. "It's been years since I've been home," he said. "I was lost, and adrift while I lived there. I need you with me, to anchor me. To remind me . . ."

"To remind you of what?" Kari asked.

"To remind me that I'm not that person anymore," Alex said.

Kari felt a lump in her throat. This man, this strong, powerful man, was saying something to her that nobody had ever said to her and she believed him. Alex was saying that he needed her. To want her was one thing. Lust was built on want. But to need her was a different ballgame. Love was built on need.

And somehow, Kari didn't fight it. He needed her, and just like he was there for Jordan, and for her so many times already, she was going to be there for him.

"It'll be my honor to go meet your family," she said.

Alex pulled her into his arms. "They're fucked up," he said. "They are not what Americans might call a Brady Bunch kind of family. But we're used to that, too."

Kari laughed. "Yes, we are," she said happily, as he held her.

CHAPTER TWENTY-FOUR

The Meet-and-Greet was held in the City Hall ballroom, and what was supposed to be an event featuring a cross-section of the community looked more like a pay-for-play on steroids. Kari, along with Faye and their friend Lucinda Mayes, the owner of a local diner where Kari sometimes worked to make ends meet, and also where she first met Alex, saw it as soon as they entered the room.

"Every big-dollar donor that's ever contributed to the mayor's campaigns are up in here," Faye said. "He's trying to run the table with these contracts."

"Sure is," Lucinda agreed. She fingered her long, blonde extensions on the right side, and then jerked it back on the left side. Although she was an attractive woman in her own right, and was always on the prowl for an attractive man, it was Faye Church, she and Kari both knew, who was the real beauty in their group.

"He's running this Meet-and-Greet like a graft operation."

"It's pay-for-play, baby," said Faye, jerking her long, brown hair back too. "You grease my palms, I'll grease yours. I sure hope Alex understands this." Then Faye and Lucinda looked at Kari.

Kari smiled. "Alex is a businessman with a worldwide company, ladies. I think he's seen his share of greedy politicians, and in bigger places than little Apple Valley. He can handle it."

Lucinda gave her a sidelong look. When Alex first hit town, Lucinda, like almost every single woman in Apple Valley, wanted to get her claws in him. She was disappointed that he didn't give her, or anybody else but Kari (to everybody's shock, including Kari's), a second glance. "So what are you saying?" she asked. "You're still down with him like that? Even after what happened with Natalie Corman?"

"Quit Lou," Faye said. "Just quit. You know I told your messy butt that it was all lies. Natalie Corman was making it all up. You know I told you that."

"I know you told me what Alex Drakos told Kari," Lucinda said. "But I don't know if that's the truth."

"It's the truth," Kari said.

"Yeah, but she's got a point, Kare," Faye said. "How do you know it's the truth?"

Kari knew Lucinda and Faye were both coming from a good place. But how do you tell your best friends that you looked into a man's eyes and decided to believe him? As simple as that? They would declare her naïve and foolish, and, worst of all, blinded by love. She wouldn't hear the last of it! "It's the truth," was all she decided to say about it. Then she added: "Let's mingle," and left their side.

Lucinda shook her head. "That girl thinks he's a saint," she said.

"I just pray she doesn't get her heart broken," said Faye.

"So do I! Because I saw Natalie Corman on one of those celebrity shows. She looked convincing to me. And that rock she wore on her finger was the real deal."

Faye nodded. "She looked convincing to me, too. But Kari believes her boo."

"But is that boo worthy of being believed? Is that boo, a man known the world over as the, quote unquote, 'billionaire playboy,' worthy of her trust?"

Faye exhaled. It was a question she couldn't answer either.

Then Lucinda looked at Faye. "I heard she's going out of the country with him," she said. "To Greece no less! He's taking her to meet his mama, Faye."

Faye nodded. "Yeah, Jordan's going to stay with us while she's gone. But dang, Lou. Who told you that already? I just found out myself last night."

"Your husband told me, matter of fact. He came by the diner this morning."

Faye smiled and shook her head. "Men love to declare that women are the big gossips, but nobody carries a bone like my hubby."

"Like your gorgeous hubby that every lady in this town would still love to have as their own man, you mean."

Faye nodded. "True that."

"At least, with Kari all into Alex right now, you don't have to worry about her anymore."

Faye looked at Lucinda. "Meaning?"

"Oh, come on, Faye! You know Benny Church always felt a little something special for Kari Grant. You had to know that."

Faye shook her head. "That's why I mind my own business and do my own thing. A man can't even be friends with a female without you thirsty-ass bitches going around declaring it something nasty. Benny loves Kari like a big brother loves a little sister, okay? They're close, and I'm glad they're close. She needed a man to help look out for her and her son in this cold world, and I'm glad my husband was that man to help her and Jordan out. Now if Alex is willing to take over the spot, then great. I'm all for that, too. But get your head out of the gutter, Lou."

"My head is not in the gutter, thank you very much."

"Yes, it is, thank you very much."

Then Lucinda paused. Faye loved her husband, and every girl in town knew that Benny was nuts about Faye. Lucinda wished she had that kind of relationship herself. "So you trust Benny like that, hun?" she asked.

"I trust Benny, yes, I do," Faye responded. "But I trust Kari more. And you and I both know Kari. If Benny come at her incorrect, she'll let me, you, and this whole town know what happened, and that it won't be happening again."

Lucinda laughed. "Now that's true. What was I thinking? Kari Grant and that mouth of hers? That is nothing but the truth!"

And it was Faye's turn to laugh.

Kari wasn't laughing, but she had a smile plastered on her face as she glad-handed colleagues and small-talked others in an effort to just make it through that Meet-and-Greet. Alex wasn't even there yet. He had separate meetings to attend all morning long, and said he would meet her there, but it had been half an hour and the guest of honor still had not shown up. The mayor even asked if she'd heard from him.

But she hadn't. And she wasn't about to try and track him down either. Given the vultures who were in that room, and how they were all friends of the mayor's rather than worthy potential vendors, she figured they could wait.

And when Alex finally did arrive, looking gorgeous, Kari thought, in his black Brook Brothers suit, she could only smile and shake her head when the vendor hopefuls began applauding him just for showing up.

Faye and Lucinda made their way over to Kari as the applause continued.

"It's suck-up time," Kari said.

"Then we'd better pucker our lips," said Faye.

"Amen," said Lucinda.

Kari looked at them. She was shocked to hear them say that. "What do you mean?"

"What do you think we mean?" Lucinda asked. "We aren't just here for our health, Kari. I want my diner to be the official caterer for his hotel."

"Yeah," said Faye, "and I want to be the official real estate broker for the employees of his hotel, and casino too. We know we're friends of yours, but we want to cash in too!"

Kari laughed. "Okay."

"Especially since you got in by the directive of none other than Alex Drakos himself," Lucinda added.

That was true. Kari had taken her company out of the running to secure a housekeeping contract with the upcoming hotel and casino, mainly because she had slept with Alex and felt it would be unfair to the other applicants who did not have that so-called "advantage." But Alex overruled her and said she was getting the contract anyway, a contract Kari knew was going to be the toughest and biggest job she'd ever undertaken. Lucinda wasn't lying. Kari was still trying to live that one down.

But it would be another half-hour of Alex doing a lot of glad-handing and small conversations himself, before he found his way to their group. He kissed Faye and Lucinda on the cheeks when he arrived. They were Kari's friends, so he took them as his friends now, too. Then he placed his arm around Kari's waist, and kissed her on the lips.

Faye and Lucinda elbowed each other. A man like Alex Drakos openly affectionate with *their* Kari was still surreal to them.

"Where's Benjamin?" Alex asked Faye.

"He has a client getting ready to go on trial," Faye responded, "and he had to attend a pre-trial hearing. He said he'd drop by if time permitted."

"He's a good attorney," said Alex. "He has a bright future in the legal profession. Remind me, Kari, to give him a call when I'm in town again. I want him on my team."

"I'll be happy to remind you," Kari said. "Faye will kill me if I don't."

They all laughed. But before Lucinda or Faye could make their pitch to join Alex's hotel and casino team, a very familiar face entered the ballroom. Faye elbowed Lucinda, and Lucinda elbowed Kari.

When Kari looked, she was as shocked as they were. "What is he doing here?" Kari asked.

"Who?" asked Alex, and looked in that direction too. "Who is he?"

"That's Paul Kurtz," Kari said. "The owner of River City Consultants."

Alex knew that name. The background he had ordered on Kari when he first met her turned up that name. "Your former boss, correct?" he asked her.

"More like her former tormentor," said Lucinda.

Alex looked at Lou. "What do you mean?"

"He was unfair in his promoting practices," Kari said. "That's what she means."

"Unfair is a kind way to put it," said Faye. "He hired hoes to sleep with, and then promoted them above Kari time and time again. Then he forced Kari to train those airheads he hired, without giving her any recognition, nor a dime increase in pay. Kari finally quit, but it was a long time coming."

Alex looked at Kari. She never seemed to catch a break. That was why it still disturbed him about that Natalie Corman situation. They were going along, smooth he thought, and then that shit hit the fan. With a lesser woman, it could have derailed them.

But Kari was willing to give him the benefit of the doubt. She was willing to hear him out, before she threw him out. And she believed him. It could have gone the other way easily for somebody accustomed to letdowns. She could have saw the signs of danger, and ran as far away as she could get from him.

But she didn't.

"He's coming over, guys," Lucinda said. "That fool is actually coming over here."

And Paul Kurtz, the owner of RCC, came over with a big grin on his face, as if all was peachy-cream and he never had a moment's ill-will toward Kari Grant.

"Mr. Drakos," he said and extended his hand, "it's an honor to meet you, sir."

Alex did not shake his hand.

But Paul, being Paul, continued to smile as he withdrew the handshake. "I just wanted to say that it's a great thing you're doing. I know you didn't have to build your casino here in Apple Valley, but you did it to help the people."

"I did it to help myself," replied Alex.

Kari could tell Paul didn't expect that reply. But Paul continued to smile anyway. "And to help yourself, of course," he said and grinned. Nobody returned his grin.

Then he turned his attention to the group. "How's everybody?" he asked, looking at the ladies. "Hey," they said dryly.

And when he turned toward Kari, his smiled increased. "Hi, Kari!" he said jovially. "Long time, no see."

Kari didn't crack a smile. Was this man for real? His actions on that job caused her all kinds of sleepless nights. And he wanted her to just forget about it?

But it was Faye, who remembered those sleepless nights too, who got to the point. "What do you want, Paul?" she asked.

"I know what he wants," Kari said. "RCC, like many of our businesses around here, are suffering in this economy. He's desperate. I can see it in his eyes. He wants his hands on one of those juicy contracts Alex has to offer. That's what he wants."

"Now that you mention it," Paul said, not too proud to beg, "I was hoping, Mr. Drakos, that you would consider my company, River City Consultants, known here in town as RCC, to become the official marketing firm of your hotel and casino. I would be honored to sit down with you and give you a brief overview."

"I'm with Kari," Alex said. "I don't think that's going to happen."

But Paul didn't seem to understand. "I will be honored to sit down with you," he said again.

Alex decided to be blunt. "I will not be honored to sit down with you," he said.

Paul understood that response, but was surprised by it. "Excuse me?"

"Kiss my ass," Alex said, to laughter from the Faye and Lucinda. "Is that clearer?"

Paul just stood there, his fat face turning red. "I was only making a business proposal, sir," he said. "I don't understand the insults."

"Was it business when you refused to promote Kari?" Alex asked. "Or was it personal? Personal between you and your whores, that is?"

Paul swallowed hard. He glanced at Kari with hate in his eyes, but then he looked back at Alex.

"My decision is personal too," Alex said. "Between you and I, that is. You will never get any contract that I am offering. Not ever. In fact, if you step foot into any business I own, including that hotel and casino, it will be the last business you step foot into. Now get the fuck out of my face."

Kari was not an eye-for-an-eye kind of person, but it felt good to see Paul chopped down to size. His disrespect and unfairness caused her to leave the best job she ever had, and it could have turned out disastrous for her. Leaving a job with no prospects for another one was never smart, and she had a kid to raise! But fools like him, Kari felt, placed women like her in tough spots like that all the time. It was his time to be in that tough spot.

Paul looked at Kari. "I'm a big man in this town," he said to her. "When your boyfriend marries that actress and has left you high and dry the way we all knows he will, then we'll see whose business is desperate. Life can get very lonely for *Maid for Mom* if I put a word out to my colleagues in this town."

"Why you nasty son-of-a-bitch," Faye said with clenched teeth, but Paul only smiled that disgusting smile and walked away. He was heading for the exit.

"What a piece of work," said Lucinda.

But if the ladies were outraged, Alex was downright livid. "I'll be back," he said to them, and was about to follow Paul.

But Kari was panic-stricken. This was still Apple Valley. She didn't want him in jail because of some idiot like Paul Kurtz. "Alex, wait," she said, grabbing him by the arm. "He's not worth it."

But Alex looked into her eyes. And his look made it clear to Kari that when it came to retribution, she was to never question any move he made. "I'll be back," he said just as forcefully, and Kari, reading him right, released his arm.

And Alex, like Paul, left the building.

But where Kari might have been distressed, Faye and Lucinda were happy. "Get the popcorn, Lou," Faye said happily, "and let's go watch the drama!"

Lucinda laughed, and she and Faye hurried behind Alex.

Kari shook her head. It was no laughing matter to her. But she followed them outside nonetheless.

But there would be no fireworks. By the time the ladies made it outside, Paul was inside of his Dodge Ram pickup truck with the window down, Alex had his arms resting on the window frame talking to Paul, and nothing, from what they could see, was going down. But Kari knew Alex. Something was going down.

And she was right. Alex was talking with Paul, alright, but only after he had grabbed Paul's hand in an apparent handshake, taken his thumb, and bent it back so far, and with such force, that it broke. And then he continued to bend it until it completely separated from the bone. Paul was in so much pain that he was sweat-filled and red as fire.

"Nobody threatens Kari Grant," were the words Alex was saying to Paul. "You threaten her ever again; if you even think about threatening her ever again, and I will not simply break your thumb. I will break every bone in your body. And then I will kill you."

Paul looked at Alex with horror in his eyes. He'd kill him just for threatening a nobody piece of shit like Kari Grant? Was he insane? Nobody would kill somebody over her!

But that look in Alex's eyes didn't lie. Paul knew what he was looking at. This man would kill him over Kari Grant! Over Kari Grant! Who was this guy?

Terror gripped Paul Kurtz. He heard all of those casino guys were as corrupt as they came, and many of them were Mafia. Was this guy, who he thought was so straight laced, one of those guys too? "I won't tell anybody," he said in a voice he knew was trembling. "I'll never, as long as I live, tell a living soul anything about our conversation. And I'll never threaten Kari ever again."

Alex smiled a smile so charming it stunned Paul. "Then off you go," Alex said, backed up from the truck, and Paul, glad to be out of the presence of such madness, sped away.

"Ah," Lucinda said, "Alex Drakos is apparently all talk, and no action."

"Nothing to see here, folks," Faye agreed, and the two ladies took their imaginary popcorn and went back into the building.

But Alex turned toward Kari, and Kari was staring at him. And they both knew better than that.

CHAPTER TWENTY-FIVE

They had only just stepped onto Alex's private plane, ready for the thirteen-hour flight to Greece, when the crew chief approached them.

"I apologize, sir," he said, "but you have a call waiting on your secure line."

Whenever Alex received those kind of calls, Kari knew he was going to take it. Although he rarely discussed his business with her to begin with, those calls made it particularly true.

And when he excused himself and headed into a room that was, even on his private plane, guarded by Security, Kari decided to mingle.

The flight crew knew her by now, and were more than happy to entertain the bubbly Floridian. What the women liked about her was how easily they could talk to her, and how she never seemed to talk down to them, nor look down on them. She, the women felt, was one of them.

What the men liked about her was the reality of her position. Alex Drakos was fucking her. She either had gold between those legs, they thought, or was golden herself. They thought this mainly because of the current trip: he'd never taken any of his other ladies to his homeland before. Not even his former wife.

By the time Kari mingled as long as she could without feeling the tiredness within her body, she retreated to Alex's bedroom. A bedroom, she still couldn't believe given that it was on a plane, that seemed as big as her house.

But this wasn't her first time at the rodeo. She knew her way around this time. She ran herself a bath in the luxurious tub, removed her clothing, and got in. She didn't even bother to lock the door because Alex's people knew, like they knew all their other duties, to never ever disturb them there.

She was able to lean her head back and relax. She never thought it would be possible the first time she got on his plane. Mainly because it was their very first date, and it was a daunting reality. Now it felt more comfortable.

With each trip, Kari felt that she was getting more comfortable. But that didn't mean, she also knew, that she was completely relaxed in his world. That, she knew, was going to take more time.

Nearly twenty minutes later, Alex came out of the room where his secure call had been conducted, anxious to see Kari again. He hated being a preoccupied host. Especially on a trip like this. So when he entered the bedroom suite, and saw her reclining in the tub, he relaxed too. Then he removed every stitch of his clothing, and got in behind her.

Although Kari's eyes remained closed when he lifted her body and got into the tub behind her, she smiled warmly. "Hurry up, Pedro," she said jokingly, "before Alex comes in."

Alex laughed. "Not even funny," he said.

"Then why did you laugh?" Kari asked him.

"You make me laugh. What can I say?"

Kari liked that answer, and leaned the back of her body against the front of his.

And what she loved about that moment, as they reclined and relaxed in the tub, was the serenity of it. Alex wasn't trying to have sex with her, although she knew he eventually would, but he was just holding her. She used to dream of a relationship like this, where a man could be satisfied just being with her. But it never happened before. Now that it was happening, and happening with a man like Alex, it was as scary as it was exciting.

"It'll be great to see your old stomping ground," she said.

"It'll be great to see yours. We must go to Miami someday."

"You've been to Miami many days."

"But only to South Beach. I wish to see that part of town you hail from."

"Sounds like a serious deflection to me."

Alex smiled. "Perceptive Kari," he said. "It was meant to be."

And it concerned Kari. He never liked to talk, in any detail, about his life when he lived in Greece. "Why?" she asked.

"My family is not your regular family."

"You've said that before. They aren't the Brady Bunch, I know. But since even the Brady Bunch probably weren't who they pretended to be either, that's no big deal to me. But what do you mean by that? Give me an example, Alex."

"My brother," he said. "His name is Odysseus."

"O-who?"

Alex spoke the name as it sounded, rather than as it was spelled: "O-DISS-SEE-US."

"Odysseus," Kari said, trying that name on for size.

"If you've ever read Homer's Odyssey or Iliad, it would ring a bell."

"It was required reading in school," Kari said. "But I didn't read it."

Alex laughed. "Okay."

"I got the name," Kari said. "But what about him?"

"That ambush Reno Gabrini spoke of?"

Kari's heart went still. "What about it?"

"I have been told that my brother, Odysseus, was behind it."

Kari leaned sideways and turned her face toward him. "Your own brother?"

"Yes."

"But . . ." She could hardly believe it. Then she realized something more. "But I thought Vito was behind that ambush," she said.

"That was what I was led to believe. Including by Vito himself. But his uncle, and it turned out to be his real uncle, was really the muscle behind it."

"But I thought," said Kari, "it was his uncle who was behind the Vegas ambush."

"Vegas, yes, and the earlier one in Florida. He was behind both. But he got his marching orders, according to him, from my brother."

"To kill you?"

"Yes."

"But why, Alex? Why would your own brother do such a thing?"

"That is why I am going to Fiskardo. To find out if he did such a thing."

"Is he capable of ordering his own brother's death?" Kari asked.

"Capable? Yes," Alex said. "It is possible that he ordered the hit. But is it probable? That I am not sure about. That's why I'm going to Fiskardo."

"Am I going to meet him while we're there?" Kari asked. She wanted to see this monster face to face.

But Alex only wrapped his arms around her, forcing her to turn back around, and he held her tighter. "We'll see," was all he would commit to.

And then she heard a phone ringing. Alex reached outside of the tub, where a platform of buttons was placed, and pressed one. "Yes?"

It was his crew chief. "It is ready for transmission, sir," he said.

"Okay," Alex responded, and then pressed a different button. Just as Kari was about to ask him what was ready for transmission, a screen dropped from its perch against the bathroom wall, and suddenly what appeared to be a YouTube broadcast was on the screen.

Kari's heart tightened when she saw that it was Natalie Corman.

"I'll make this short and sweet," Natalie said. It appeared to be her and a camera, and she was facing the camera head on. "When I made the announcement that Alex Drakos had proposed to me, I thought everybody would understand that it was nothing but a joke. But, to my horror, people took me seriously."

She attempted to smile it off, but Kari only saw fear in her eyes, and embarrassment. "It wasn't true, folks, okay? I was joking around! I've only dated Alex Drakos a couple of times, and that was it. No on-again, off-again relationship. Nothing. We are not engaged, okay? That engagement ring was something I purchased because I feel women should empower themselves."

"No that heifer isn't trying to turn her lies into women's rights," Kari said, staring at the screen.

"Yes, that heifer is," Alex responded, staring at the screen.

"So, I say to everybody who believed me, you have to remember how good an actress I am." She smiled after saying that.

Kari shook her head. "Do these people have any morals?" she asked.

"None," responded Alex. "If I would not have threatened to sue her ass and expose her myself, her charade would have continued."

"And to Mr. Drakos," Natalie Corman continued, "I say that I owe you an apology, sir, and I apologize profusely. I did not mean to hurt you nor your loved ones with my flippancy. Please forgive me."

And then she was out. And the screen went black.

"Lying motherfucker," Alex said.

Kari turned toward him again. "Is that enough for you?" she asked.

But Alex looked at her and reversed the question. "Is that enough for *you*?" he asked.

Kari nodded. "I could have done without the women's empowerment line, but yes. Yes, it is. But you know people are going to believe whatever they want to believe anyway."

"You are correct about that," Alex agreed. He stared at Kari. He loved her sincere eyes. "I'm sorry it ever happened," he said.

"I know you are," Kari said heartfelt, and they continued to stare at each other.

It only took seconds before the look in Alex's eyes began to change. Kari saw it first, and then she felt it beneath her. His cock began to harden and expand. And suddenly she felt as if she was sitting on steel.

Alex lifted her body, easily for him, and then placed that steel pole between her legs. He held his dick head, and began rubbing it against her clit.

Kari leaned her head back onto his broad shoulder, and closed her eyes.

"Feels good?" Alex asked her, as he took a finger and began fingering her too.

"Yes," she said, feeling those feelings with great satisfaction.

And when he turned and lifted her body in a position that his mouth was able to reach her breasts, he began sucking her too. It felt like a three-prone attack to Kari. An attack so sensual, and so wonderful, that she arched her back and gave Alex complete access. He could have any part of her body he wanted!

And Alex took every part of her body. He removed his lips from her breasts and kissed her on the mouth with a long, passionate kiss. Then he was sucking her breasts again. And still fingering her. And still rubbing, with his dick head, her clit.

Until he took that same dick head, and slid it into her wetness.

She was so wet, and so ready, that he was able to go all the way in with one push. And he let out a loud sigh himself when he was all the way in.

And then they were fucking. She was riding him, and he was riding her, and they were off.

Slap sounds. Sounds of juices intermingling. Moans and groans echoed throughout that bathroom and all of his bedroom suite. Kari's stomach was pushed in, and her ass was protruded out, as Alex fucked her so hard that she thought he was going to tear open her insides.

But there was no tearing. Just loving. And Alex loved on her for a long, sensual ride.

And when they came, they came together. Alex and Kari. And it was such a hard cum that his release filled Kari up, and then spilled out into the tub.

CHAPTER TWENTY-SIX

When the plane touched down in Kefalonia, Greece, a team of cars were waiting to escort them to the village of Fiskardo. Kari, waiting on Alex, was ready to go. Alex was on the phone, but then he concluded his call and was ready to go too. Or so Kari thought. Because as soon as she thought they were ready to deplane, Alex stopped her.

"Wait here," he said to her.

She waited. She watched through the windows on the plane as Alex went down to the waiting cars, spoke with a man she assumed was in charge of the entourage, and then headed back toward the plane. As he did, the cars behind him began leaving the airstrip.

Kari was shocked. She glanced at the flight crew, to see if they were shocked, too, and she could tell that they were. Everybody looked at Alex when he walked back onto the plane.

Kari had so many questions, and she knew the crew was leaving it up to her to ask them, but she held her peace. Alex's eyes had all but told her when they were at that Meet-and-Greet in Apple Valley that when he made a decision regarding security or, in that case, *retribution*, she was not to question that decision publicly. She did not question it, and he did not offer any explanation. This was his world she was in, and she had to trust that he knew how to live in it far better than she.

And just as she was thinking it, another group of cars drove up. And somehow, Kari could tell that those cars, unlike the former ones that undoubtedly belonged to his father, were Alex's team. Kari could see his entire demeanor change, when those cars pulled up.

And as the cars assembled, Alex went into his bedroom, retrieved a leather bomber jacket from his wardrobe, and went over to Kari. "Put this on," he was saying even as he was already putting it on her. "It's chilly outside."

Kari didn't argue with him, although she already had on a cardigan sweater to go along with her slacks and tucked-in blouse. She didn't even complain when the jacket, because it belonged to big Alex, swamped her.

He held onto the collar as he snuggled her into his jacket. For a moment, it seemed as if he was having second thoughts about bringing her to his home turf. Did he want her to stay onboard and let the plane take her back to Florida? If he did, Kari wasn't all that certain if she would object.

But it wasn't to be. Alex was not the kind of man to make a decision, and then waffle. "Ready?" he asked her.

Kari was still nervous about meeting his family, especially given his sudden hesitancy, but she nodded. She didn't want him worrying about her, too. "Completely," she said.

They got off of the plane and made their way across the tarmac. Alex kept his arm on the small of Kari's back, and continually looked around, until they got to the first car. He placed her on the passenger seat, and then got in behind the wheel.

Kari was surprised. She expected the head of the security detail, a man Alex called Cronos when they arrived at the car, to drive. But Cronos, instead, got in the backseat. Alex was driving. Kari held her peace there, too. This was Alex's world, and she could tell before this journey even began that it was going to be a different world.

Fiskardo was a fishing village within the northernmost port of Kefalonia, surrounded by the sea and mountains. And as they made the hour-and-a-half drive to town, Kari actually enjoyed the view. There was a calm to this region of Greece. There was a sense that she was entering, not a backward old world, but an almost strange new world. This could not have been truer when Alex drove up a steep mountain that led to a compound that was completely walled off.

More than ten men, as Kari counted them, were standing at the gate of the compound with high-powered rifles. They walked up to the first car in the entourage of cars, and Alex pressed down the window. But when the men saw who was behind the wheel, they all grinned and shook his hand.

"*O Assos einai piso!*" one of them yelled. "*O Assos einai piso!*" The other men began hurrying to the car. "*O Alexio einai piso!*"

"What are they saying?" Kari asked.

"Ace is back," said Alex, as he smiled broadly and shook their hands. "Alexio is back."

They were smiling, too, as he greeted all of his former subordinates, and then the heavy gates opened, and they drove on through. Kari might have been visiting in this world, she thought, but Alex seemed completely at home.

As the entourage made its way through the winding driveway that led to the main house, Kari was struck at how it appeared as a medieval castle perched on the edge of the sea. Very gothic in its appearance. Very foreboding and grim.

Kari also noticed how Alex's smile dissipated the closer they got to the castle. A group was waiting for him at the top of the stairs. A group that consisted of an attractive older couple - male and female, and a younger female who could be Kari's age.

A huge staff of what appeared to be uniformed maids and butlers were also lined up, facing each other, ready to greet Alex. They were smiling and appeared excited, and when Alex looked at them, he was smiling too. But when Alex looked at the top of the stairs where the threesome stood, Kari noticed, his smile disappeared.

As soon as their car stopped, one of the servants immediately hurried over and opened Alex's door. Although Kari was so anxious to get out of that car and eyeball these people for herself, she knew to remain in the car and wait. Alex always, but always opened the car door for her, and she wasn't about to get him off stride here. He liked treating her like a queen, she could tell. And, if truth be told, she liked being treated that way.

Alex got out, smiled at the doorman and the other servants, and walked around and opened the car door for Kari. It was only then did Cronos, in the backseat, get out too.

"Hold my hand," Alex whispered to Kari as soon as she stepped out of the car, "and don't let it go."

Kari was surprised to hear him say that. She didn't know if such an odd request was for her protection, or his! But either way, it was fine with her. She'd rather hold onto Alex's hand than any other man's alive. "Okay," she whispered back.

As they made their way between the line of servants, Alex felt like the prodigal son. It had been years since he stepped foot in this place. Years! But it felt like it did the day he packed up and left. There was a suffocation. An isolation. And a desolation that he could never explain. He hated it here. But he knew he had to bear it. He was just glad he had Kari by his side.

He and Kari's hands were tightly clutched as the servants smiled and nodded at them as they made their way toward the stairs. Kari and Alex smiled and nodded back, at each and every one of them, and Kari could tell they were genuinely happy to see Alex again. A couple of the older ladies even broke protocol and hugged Alex. Alex gave them a big hug back. Kari glanced upstairs. The older woman, especially, did not seem pleased.

But then there was another break from protocol. The young woman that appeared to be around Kari's age, broke away from the older couple and began running down the stairs toward Alex. And she was smiling grandly.

Although Alex smiled, too, when he saw her, Kari could tell it didn't contain the same warmth he displayed with the help. It seemed genuine, but painful too.

"Alexio!" she was yelling as she came. "Alexio!" And she fell into Alex's arms.

"Hello, Zylena," Alex said with a much more muted smile. "How are you?"

"Much better," she said in perfect English, "now that you have arrived. You know how they are! How are you?"

Alex, no liar, didn't answer that question. He, instead, turned to Kari. "I want you to meet my lady. This is Karena Grant. Karena, this is my baby sister."

"Hi," Kari said with a smile, extending her hand.

Although Zylena shook the hand, her eyes were still on her brother. "I thought I heard you were going to marry Natalie Corman. The actress, no? She does not look like Natalie Corman."

"Natalie told a lie," Alex said.

"I heard that too," said his sister.

"Then why did you repeat it?"

"Just having a bit of fun with you," the sister said with a smile, and although Kari smiled, too, Alex didn't.

"Come on," Zylena said, grabbing her brother by his arm. But when Alex would not let go of Kari's hand, she moved over to his free arm, grabbed it, and began pulling him toward the stairs. "Let's go see the parents," she said.

And she, Alex, and Kari made their way up the stairs.

Kari had suspected that the older, attractive couple were Alex's parents, so that was no surprise. But the chill even she could feel as they approached them was.

And when they made it to the top, and Alex was standing right in front of the two people who brought him into this world, their chill was nothing compared to his. "Hello, Mother. Hello, Father."

His father, at least, cracked a small smile. His mother never did. "Hello, son," he said. He, too, spoke perfect English. "It is good to have you back home where you belong."

Alex didn't respond to that. Instead, he looked at his mother. She was staring at Kari. *"Poio einai auto to atomo?"*

Kari looked at Alex. "'Who is this person', she said."

"It's not Natalie Corman, I will tell you that!" Zylena said, with a grin.

"This is Karena Grant," Alex said to his mother, who, like his entire family, spoke fluent English. "My girlfriend."

It was the first time Alex had been that explicit in his description of his relationship with Kari. Usually, she was his lady. Now she was his girlfriend. It sounded like an elevation to Kari, although she could not be sure if it was an elevation for show, or for sure.

"Kari, these are my parents, Elasaid and Leda Drakos."

"Hello," Kari said. The mother might be rude, but Kari was not going to be as well.

"Hello," the mother responded, to Kari's surprise. It was more than she had responded to her own son. Then the mother looked at Alex with a look Kari could only describe as hurt laced with bitterness. "Let's go inside," she said, and turned and headed inside.

The father opened the door for the rest of them, and Kari, and then Zylena, and then Alex walked on in.

Kari tried her best not to be blown away by the massiveness of the house. Everything about it was HUGE. But also cold and sterile too. Just as chilly, Kari thought, as she had felt outside.

Kari, in fact, snuggled even more into Alex's big bomber jacket as they all settled into a room that could only be described as a combination living room and bar. A massive, restaurant-styled bar in the back of the room, with a complete staff behind its massive counter.

"What would you care to drink, madam? Sir?" It was apparently the bartender, who had come over and spoke to Kari and Alex.

"What would you like, babe?" Alex asked Kari.

"Sherry would be nice."

Alex looked at the bartender, a man he did not know. "A Sherry for the lady," he said, "a gin and tonic for me."

"Right away, sir," the bartender ordered, clapped his hands, and then one of the men behind the bar began making the drinks. The bartender left to retrieve them.

But even after the drinks were served, and everybody seemed to settle down, there was no urgent discussion whatsoever. Everything seemed like small talk to Kari.

"How is the weather in New York?" the father asked Alex.

"It's okay," responded Alex.

"I want to go to New York," said the sister. "But Alexio won't invite me."

"Have you asked him?" the father asked.

"Countless times."

"His excuse?"

"He's busy. He does not have time. It's insulting."

"Yes, it is," said the mother. "But that's your brother."

"Why so much security?" Alex asked.

It was the first real question, Kari thought.

"Well," said the father. "You know how that goes."

"No, Father, I do not. Enlighten me."

"You are not here by accident. That is what I feel about it," said his father. "You are here by providence!"

"Spare me the dramatics, Father," Alex said boldly. He knew his father too well. "Why so much security?"

"It is needed," Elasaid replied. "You know what I am talking about. You have not been that far removed from your own family, although you have made it your life's calling to do so. What do you think I do for a living, Alexio? What do you think? You think I sell pita bread? Or preowned vehicles? Or boats?"

"You have done all of that," Alex said, "and more."

His father actually smiled, which made him, Kari thought, appear quite charming. "Yes, I have!" Then the smile was gone. "But no more. I have a family to support. I have an organization to support. That is why the increased security. That is why we are living like prisoners in our own home!"

A war, Alex thought. His father was all but telling him that he was in the midst of a war with one of the families. There were only five major ones that ruled the entirety of Greece. His father's syndicate was the biggest, but perhaps no longer the *baddest*, after Alex left.

"What did you do?" Alex asked Elasaid.

"Why do you assume it is always me? I fly, how do they say it in America? Under the radar. I make it my business to fly under the radar. But they still force my hand. They still put me in these positions from which I am unable to free! I have never started anything. You know that, Alexio. You know how I ran my business. That has not changed because you left us. That has not changed because you turned your back on us. I still run my business well, and under the radar. They keep coming for me!"

Although his father sounded sincere, Alex knew him too well. He had a temper that, when uncontrolled, was deadly to a degree Alex had never seen before. But did he want details? No. He was not getting involved.

"Are you marrying her then?" asked his kid sister, and everybody looked at her. Where did that come from?

"What?" Alex asked her. He frowned and appeared, it seemed to Kari, to have very little patience with her.

"This one here, this Karena Grant," Zylena said, "are you going to marry her the way I thought you were going to marry Natalie Corman?"

But it was Kari who answered her. "We're still getting to know each other," she said. Alex tightened his grip on her hand. He wished she would not have said that.

And, as he knew she would, his mother came out with the knives. "Still getting to know each other?" she asked. "You bring a woman to our home whom you do not know?"

"That's not what she meant," Alex responded.

"That is what she said."

"I don't give a fuck what she said," Alex said to his mother so harshly that Kari herself was shocked, even though he was defending her. "That is not what she meant."

And his mother showed her displeasure with him, too. "You are now and always will be a bastard. Have your own daughter arrested. Murder your own son."

"I did not murder my son!" Alex yelled.

"So say you! But Linda told us what happened. That suicide claim was a fake, she said. You murdered poor Jonathan because he stole a little money from you! She told it all!"

Alex was so tired of people lying on him that he didn't know how to contain his anger. He was about to unload, but he glanced at Kari and saw the terror in her eyes. He held back. "She told you lies," he said to his mother. "But believe my bitter ex-wife over me if you care to. It would be exactly as expected. I had no idea you and she were such friends. You never wanted to meet her once while we were married."

"But that was before she and Odysseus," Zylena started to say, but caught herself.

Kari looked at Zylena. Why didn't she continue?

Alex was equally curious. "What about Linda and Odysseus?" Alex asked his sister.

But his mother intervened. "Is that his business?" she asked Zylena. "Tell me where, under this Hellenistic sun, is that his business?"

"What were you about to say, Zylena?" Alex asked her.

But then the front door flew open as if a strong wind had blown it open, and everybody looked in that direction. Alex even released Kari's hand and stood to his feet. And if things weren't already tense and unsettling, it all rose to new heights instantaneously.

Odysseus Drakos, the man believed to be behind those attempts on Alex's life, along with Kari's in Vegas, suddenly and dramatically walked in.

CHAPTER TWENTY-SEVEN

Kari didn't know who he was. All she saw was the front door fly open and a larger-than-life character almost as tall as Alex, and almost as big as he, walked in. And although it was a cool day in Fiskardo to a point where Alex made Kari put on one of his jackets before they left the plane, this guy wore a full-length fur coat and a big-rimmed, stylish hat. He also had a cigar between his teeth and entered grinning.

Alex had already risen to his feet, and so had his father, but it wasn't until Zylena broke away from the group and ran toward the door yelling, *"Oz is home! Odysseus is home!"* that Kari realized who he was. He was Alex's younger brother. He was the man who might have been responsible for that ambush in Vegas, and the earlier attempt, in Florida, on Alex's life. Kari rose to her feet, too.

Unlike Alex before him, Odysseus Drakos hugged his baby sister vigorously. It appeared to Kari, after only just laying eyes on him, that he was the kind of man who did EVERYTHING vigorously.

And then he, and Zylena, made their way to them.

Also, unlike Alex, Odysseus went over, removed his cigar from his mouth, and kissed their mother on the cheek. Their mother, for the very first time in Kari's presence, actually smiled. He was apparently her favorite.

"How are you, Mother?" he asked her.

"I am wonderful," she said as if she wasn't the gloomy person she presented herself to be earlier. "You?"

Odysseus stood erect. "Good."

"I heard not good. I heard drunk and disorderly in town last night."

"Don't believe everything you hear. I've never been disorderly a day in my life."

"Ha!" his mother responded, not believing him for a second. "Tell that to the birdies," she added.

But then Odysseus nodded at his father, but turned his attention to their guests. To Alex and Kari. He left Zylena's side, who was still clinging to him, and walked over to his big brother. They were now face to face.

"So you made it," he said to Alex. "Papa said you were coming, but I had to see it to believe it." Then he looked at Kari. "And to bring such a beautiful lady with you."

He smiled at Kari. "I am Odysseus," he said to her, "but I am also known as Oz. As in the Wizard of? As in the man who can make all your dreams come true?"

His charming was contagious and Kari would have smiled if she didn't know his backstory. But she knew his backstory. She remained stoic.

"I know what you're thinking," Oz continued. "And the answer is yes, you are correct! We have so little life in this forsaken land that we are movie buffs here. English is our first language, as it is fluently spoken by more than half the village. Greek spoken only where needed. That is the strangeness of Fiskardo." Then he grinned and extended his hand. "So nice to meet you."

He was charming as hell, Kari thought, with those kind of ruggedly good looks ladies undoubtedly loved, although Kari wasn't crazy about it. But she did not shake his hand. If this man did what Alex was told he had done, it would be like shaking the hands of your tormenter.

But Oz, being smooth as silk, Kari thought, didn't withdraw his hand. He merely turned it toward Alex, and extended it to him. "Hello, brother," he said.

But Alex didn't shake his hand, either, forcing him to drop it. His parents might have kowtowed to him. But Alex didn't.

"It was really wrong what you did to Linda, big brother," Oz said, seemingly out of the blue.

Kari and Alex looked at him.

"Oh, yes," Oz said, "I know about that. The idea of harming such a beautiful face. To shame, Alexio! But no worries. She is working with a plastic surgeon. She'll be back to being her beautiful self in no time!"

"You know an awfully lot about the woman," said Elasaid, Alex's father.

But Oz would only smile about that.

Fuck Linda, Alex thought. It was high time to get down to business. "Did you order those attempts on my life?" he asked his brother.

Oz was grinning again. "A pointblank person," he said. "You have not changed a bit, big brother."

"Did you order those attempts on my life?" Alex asked again.

"That would be a rude question," Alex's father chimed in, "if it turns out to be untrue."

"True, untrue," said Leda, the mother. "What does Alexio care? He left us when we needed him most."

"But he is back," said Oz, "when we need him even more."

"Answer my question, Odysseus," Alex said. "Were you the man who gave the order?"

Oz stared at his older brother. And then he nodded. "Yes," he said.

When he affirmed that it was true, Kari expected shockwaves to reverberate throughout that household. But they all looked if it was no news to them.

The father, at least, acknowledged the strangeness of it. "I told Odysseus that it was not good form," he said, "but he did it anyway."

Not good form, Kari wanted to say. Ordering his brother's assassination was not good form? Was he for real?

But Alex didn't give his father's comment a second thought. His only focus was his brother. "Why?" he asked him. "Why would you do such a thing?"

And for the first time, Kari could see pain in Alex's eyes. Before she could not read the depth of emotion she was seeing in his troubled eyes. But now it was clear. His brother had not only betrayed him, but had hurt him to his core. There was a time, Kari believed, when Alex and Odysseus had been close.

But Oz reverted to his natural habitat, and smiled once again. "You are needed here," he said. "I could not think of any other way to get you here."

Alex was as shocked as Kari. "You couldn't think of any other way?" he asked. "Speak plainly!" he added.

"I ordered those attacks," said Oz, "knowing full well that you would survive them."

Kari could not believe it. She could hold her peace no longer. What he had just spoken begged the question. "And if he didn't survive those attacks?" she asked Oz angrily, and everybody, except Alex, looked at her.

Oz, especially, was taken aback by her spunk. Who was she to question him? But he liked spunk and could not dismiss her. "If he did not survive," he said in his usual deadpan way, "then he would no longer be the man he used to be, and would be of no use to us anyway."

But as Kari absorbed the shock of that statement, Oz had a different problem on his hand. Alex's heart was already filled with rage. Now, with that statement, it was overflowing with rage that Alex could no longer contain.

Before anybody saw it coming, Alex took his sizeable fist and slammed it into the side of his brother's face.

Oz stumbled back, as his cigar went one way and his hat went the other way. He looked at Alex. He was shocked by the hit.

But Alex showed no mercy. He grabbed his brother and began punching him and punching him. Oz grabbed his brother, fighting back, and they both fell over a table, breaking it.

"That is enough, Alexio!" his father was yelling.

"Do something, Elasaid!" yelled his mother.

"A fight! A fight!" yelled his silly sister.

And the fight was on.

But Alex proved why he was the king of the mountain when he lived on that mountain. He beat Oz's ass. Kari could not have been prouder of her man. Alex beat Oz from one end of that room, to the other end. Everybody was on their feet. Nobody could believe the rage Alex held within him.

"Karena was with me, you asshole!" he was yelling at his brother as he grabbed him up from the floor once more, and continued to pound on him. "Kari was with me!" Blood was everywhere, but he kept on beating him. "She could have been killed, you crazy fuck! She could have been killed!"

But something else shocked Kari: Alex's father had changed his tune. Instead of trying to break up the fight, or urge his sons to cut it out even more, Elasaid began chanting, *that's my boy, that's my boy*, over and over, as if he was in a trance. Alex was making Elasaid proud too. He had never had a member of his syndicate as vicious as Alex could be. That was why he was thrilled that Odysseus had gotten him back home. Alex had that killer instinct. He had what it took to take them all out just like he was taking out his own brother.

But when Alex was on his knees, continuing to plummet his nearly unconscious brother, it was Kari who knew she had to intervene. It was one thing to beat his brother's ass. That bastard deserved every lick, in Kari's view. But did Alex really want his brother's death on his hand?

She went to Alex, and placed her hands on his shoulders. "You're going to kill him, Alex," she said to him. "You're going to kill him!"

It was only then, on hearing Kari's voice, was Alex able to get out of that dangerous zone, and come back to himself.

He stopped beating his unresponsive brother. But he remained there, staring at his brother. And then rose to his feet.

His mother and sister, now horrified by what they had just witnessed, ran to Oz's aid.

Elasaid, however, had been so mesmerized by Alex's pure power, and the fact that his oldest child still had that instinct in him, that he, too, was shocked to realize that it had gone this far.

"Everybody to their quarters," the father said. "This is enough for one afternoon. Meet back, at seven, for dinner." He looked at Alex. "Then we will talk business," he said, and left the room.

Oz was being helped to his feet by his mother and sister. He looked at Alex, through nearly swollen eyes, and smiled, even as his own blood had trickled onto his pearly whites. "You're the only man alive who could have done this to me," he said. "That was why I made that order. You're the only man who can help us."

And then Oz, a mighty warrior in his own right, allowed the ladies to help him out of the room.

Kari was staring at Alex. Was he ready to leave this hellish place? He got his revenge. Was he ready to go? His father and brother were behaving as if they knew he wouldn't leave them high and dry. They were talking as if they knew he would be there for dinner, when business, as his father called it, would be discussed. Kari didn't know Alex like they knew Alex. She wasn't at all sure about what he would do. Stay and help this family, a family who didn't deserve his help, or get the hell out while he could?

"Come on," Alex said to Kari as he placed his hand around her waist, and escorted her out of that room too.

CHAPTER TWENTY-EIGHT

The Drakos estate was high up in the mountains and Alex and Kari's villa had a breathtaking view of the Ionian Sea. Kari sat on the window seat of the floor-to-ceiling window, sipping tea, and mesmerized by the view. She didn't think she'd ever seen anything more beautiful. She had on a bathrobe. She had just gotten out of the shower. While Alex, with more than mere travel dirt to clean off of him, was still in the tub.

It was turning into an arduous trip. This family was so messed up that Kari wondered if she wanted any parts of it. From the father on down, it seemed as if they only wanted Alex there to use him for their twisted purpose. Whatever that purpose was.

She could hear Alex, in the adjacent bathroom, get out of the tub. It would be a little more time, however, before Alex would enter the room. And when he walked in, drying off his naked body, Kari couldn't help it.

Seeing his tall, athletic body; seeing his cock just dangling there in all its brilliance and size even in its unaroused state, caused her vagina to pulsate.

"Enjoying the view?" Alex asked her.

Kari smiled, still staring at his fine ass. "Very much," she said.

Alex smiled too. "I mean *that* view," he asked, motioning toward the window.

Kari laughed, and looked back out of the window. "That view too," she said. "Very much."

Alex tossed the towel away and walked up to her, staring out at the magnificence of their surroundings. He leaned against the massive windowpane as he looked out.

"You grew up around all of this beauty?" Kari asked him.

"Born and raised," he said.

"Wow," said Kari. "Just wow. This might just be too beautiful for me to take every single day. If *too beautiful* is even a phrase."

"It is a phrase," Alex said, still staring out. "But I loved it. I would even escape to it late at night."

"Escape to it?" Kari asked. "How?"

Alex smiled. "Through an escape route behind the sink in the bathroom of this very villa, a passage that my parents did not know existed. I happened upon it by accident myself. But I would sit at the sea for hours on end, just staring at the waves. So yes, it was never too beautiful for me. It was the only beauty there was in this place. It certainly wasn't in our hearts or minds. We were heartless people. Our minds were singularly focused."

Kari looked at him. Alex heartless? "Singularly focused on what?" she asked him.

Alex paused as if he wasn't going to answer that question. But then he did. "Keeping our family alive," he said. "But yes, this beauty was needful, given the ugliness around me."

"Does that ugliness include your brother?" Kari asked.

"Not at first, no. After I decided I wanted nothing more to do with these people, he was the most upset. The most hurt. We were very close once upon a time, you see." Alex exhaled and a distressed look appeared in his eyes.

Kari took his hand. "You did what you had to do, Alex," she said. "Or should I call you Alexio?"

Alex gave off a weak smile. "That is my actual name."

"Alexio? Really? Not Alexander?"

"In America, it is Alexander. They have a fascination with Alexander the Great, the greatest Greek who ever lived, so I went with it. But at birth it was Alexio."

"Which do you prefer?" Kari asked.

"I don't care for either name, to tell you the truth," Alex said, and Kari laughed.

But then the laughter died back down. And Kari looked at him again. "How could he do that to you?" she asked. "He said he knew you'd survive it, but how did he know that?"

"He knows me. And what I'm capable of."

Kari felt a sudden surge of nervousness. There was a side of Alex that she saw earlier, when he nearly took his brother away from this life, that did disturb her, if she were to be honest. "What are you capable of, Alex?" she asked him pointedly.

On that question, Alex didn't hesitate. "I was my father's number two," he said, "before I gave it all up. My father is considered the most powerful man in Greece. At least, in the underworld, or underbelly as it really should be called. I am capable of your worst nightmare, Kari," he admitted. "Times twelve."

Kari's chest constricted. She attempted to drink more tea, but Alex, seeing her distress, took her hand and pulled her to her feet. He then took her cup and set it aside, and pulled her into his arms.

Although they were close, and she could feel his penis jut against her bathrobe, they were far enough apart in their upper bodies that they could look into each other's eyes. "I left this world behind because of what it turned me into," he said. "I went to America and made my fortune there. I will never go back to that life again."

"But your brother said they need you."

"I know what my brother said. They are always saying that. I stopped listening after many years. You stop listening too."

Kari gave a smile, but it was weak at best. She was still concerned. But she didn't want Alex worrying about her too. "Okay," she said.

But Alex was worried about her. He was worried that she would see this side of him, and recoil enough that she would eventually, when they returned to the States, recoil forever. And that, for Alex, would be the tragedy of this whole trip. But if she was going to be with him, he also knew, she had to know who she was being with.

They stared into each other's eyes. They stared long enough that, although their loving gaze didn't change, their motives did. Their needs did. Because sex for Alex and Kari, at this early stage in their relationship, was not about stress relief or pure lust. It was about reaffirming to each other that this was what they wanted. That this was what they needed. And when Alex leaned down and kissed her, and then began untying her robe, they both were about to show that being with each other was what they had to have.

With Kari's robe opened, exposing her own naked body, Alex lifted her onto the window sill itself, with her back to that view they both adored, as he opened her legs, knelt down, and began eating her.

With the backdrop of the sea hitting against rocks and raging around them, as if it were a metaphor for the turmoil that they both knew they still had to face, Alex did not spare her. He ate her with a passion that caused Kari's heart to hammer, stomach to pump in and out, and face to blush with ecstasy.

And Alex's heart was hammering too, as he licked her harder and harder and forced his tongue into her deeper and deeper. He ate her so hard, and with so much passion that he had Kari butted against the window sill, with her legs on his back. Her hands were outstretched and pressed against the window frame, as if she wanted to get away from the intensity because it felt almost too wonderful, in that same way their view was too beautiful, but she couldn't pull herself away.

And when Alex stood up, and, like a sudden flashflood, rammed his cock into her, pushing it all the way in to the tip of his balls, filling her entire space with its size and hardness, Kari began to breath with short, uneasy breaths. Sweat appeared on the tip of her nose. And when Alex began to move inside of her, causing her considerable pain because of his size, she endured that initial hurt. But when the pain gave way to those great feelings, as he kept stroking her in a space too tight for stroking, she nearly passed out. It felt that good!

And it made for a heady sight, far away from that mountain, with the sea bearing witness to the great Alexio Drakos fucking his woman hard right in front of it, in plain view, without giving a second thought to hiding. Or to curbing even an ounce of the enormous appetite he had for his lady.

And when Alex came, he shot a wad deep inside of Kari, causing her to have a hot, trembling cum. And then he shot an equally big wad against that windowpane, as if to strut his stuff; as if to show to that sea that that painful place of his former life did not break him yet.

As if to rub it in.

CHAPTER TWENTY-NINE

Alex's mother sat her napkin on her lap and exhaled. "We always have to wait for him. It is as if he runs things. I don't know why Elasaid is so solicitous."

"Be kind, Leda," said Jabari Drakos. He was one of the two new faces that sat at the dinner table. Both were Elasaid's brothers. "We need him."

"After what he did to Odysseus?" Leda responded. "I do not see why!"

Odysseus was at the table too, wearing dark shades now, and did not comment. His father, however, was smiling. "Alexio put Oz in his place. Something I have been trying to do for some time now. There is nothing wrong in that."

"I am in agreement with Leda," said Maximus Drakos, Elasaid's younger brother. "We can handle this, with the right strategy. To dredge him up from America seems excessive to me. Where is he now, anyway?"

"He's so busy fucking that black girl, he doesn't have time for his own family," Leda said. "And that's the only reason he wants her: to fuck her."

Jabari smiled. "That can't be the only reason, Leda," he said, "or he would not have brought her here."

"The only reason!" Leda said forcefully. "What else does Alexio want with any woman? And to bring that one to my home! At least Linda came from a good family, and he would never bring her here. But from what I've discovered about the black girl, she is pure *porni*! She was underprivileged. She came from a horrid family. She had a child when she was but fifteen years old!"

"So did Zylena," Oz said quietly. "But, of course, we do not talk about that. Appearances, appearances. Right, Mother? As the first family of Fiskardo, and all of the Greek underworld, we must keep up appearances." He looked at his mother. "At least the American kept hers."

The room went still when Oz tossed that grenade, and when they heard footsteps on the stairs it became more of a chance to move on, than a chance to admonish Alex for his tardiness.

And when Alex arrived in the dining hall, with Kari at his side, the entire family, including Oz, and even Leda, rose to their feet. Kari was surprised by such a gesture.

She was still feeling the effects of Alex's enormous sexual appetite, not to mention his enormous penis, and was pleasantly drained, but drained nonetheless, from the hard, sexual beating he had just put on her.

That was why she was glad to lean against him, not only for clarity as they made their way toward the table, but for strength. "Why are they standing?" she asked him.

"I was my father's number two in command," Alex responded. "You stand for father, and his number two. It is meant to show respect."

"They respect you that much, even though you're no longer the number two?" Kari asked.

"They need me that much," replied Alex. "They want me to return to being his number two."

Kari didn't like the sound of that, but after what she witnessed him doing to his brother earlier, she understood why they would want to pull out the stops to get a man like Alex back. Alex said it wasn't going to work; that there was no way he was going back in, and she prayed he was able to keep his word.

"Welcome home, Nephew," said Jabari happily. "So great to see you again! And I see you have a guest with you. A beautiful, American guest."

"Let's not overstate the matter, Jabari," Alex's mother chimed in. "American, yes. Beautiful?" She rocked her hand from side to side. "*Eh.*"

Kari heard the slight, but ignored it. That woman just wanted to get a rise out of them. She was pleased that Alex understood what she was doing and ignored it, too.

Although Elasaid sat at the head of the table furthest away from the entrance, Alex's seat was reserved at the head of the table nearest the entrance. He and Kari stood there.

"Please introduce us," Jabari said.

"This is my girlfriend, Karena Grant," Alex said to his uncle. "Kari," he said to his woman, "these are my uncles: Jabari and Maximus Drakos."

Kari smiled and nodded in their direction. "Nice to meet you."

"Very nice to meet you," said Jabari.

Maximus only nodded back at her.

And then Alex sat Kari down in the empty chair to the right of his chair, and then he sat down at the head of the table. The rest of the family sat down, too.

"Elasaid is always telling us how well you are doing in America," Jabari said. "He says you made your fortune and never looked back. I read about you in the magazines." He grinned. "The billionaire playboy, eh?"

"Have you ever known me to play, Uncle Jabari?" Alex asked him.

Jabari laughed. "No indeed! Odysseus? All the time. You? Never!"

Elasaid and Maximus joined in the laughter. Alex smiled too. He and his uncle used to be two of the biggest players in Greece, and they all knew Jabari was only kidding.

Although Kari didn't know this history, she, for one, was happy to see Alex smile. It was one of the few genuine smiles she had seen him express since their arrival in Fiskardo.

"Now," said Elasaid, picking up a bell by his side and tinkling it, "let's eat!"

Immediately the servants arrived from the kitchen with bowls of food as if they had been standing on the other side of the door waiting for the bell. And dinner was served.

But after dinner, Alex knew they would get down to business. His uncles Jabari and Maximus never broke bread with the family unless there was family business to discuss. Both worked for Elasaid, but neither were particularly in love with their oldest brother's management style. Getting down to the brass tacks time, Alex thought, was going to be difficult. But it occurred as soon as the meal had been eaten.

Alex was still dabbing his mouth with his napkin when Elasaid looked at him. "Perhaps the women would prefer to go into the drawing room?" he asked.

Kari found such a request objectionable in and of itself, but she didn't have to speak it. Alex did for her. "Whatever you have to say, you may say it in front of Karena. She is well aware of what our family is about."

"But it is one thing to know about our family," Elasaid responded. "It is another thing to know about our family's activities. Unless," he added, "you are telling us here and now that she is going to be a permanent part of our family."

Kari's heart began to pound. She didn't even look Alex's way. How in the world, she wondered, would he respond to that?

"Whatever you have to say," was all Alex would respond, "you may say it in front of Karena."

For a small part of Kari, it was a bit of a letdown to be sure. But for the bigger part of her, she was glad Alex wasn't ready to go that far. Because, in truth, she wasn't ready either. Besides, this family, in her opinion, didn't deserve to be the first to know their future plans anyway.

But that very family saw it differently. The fact that Alexio told them to carry on, meant an elevation for Kari in their eyes. It meant, as they saw it, that she was no ordinary piece of ass to Alexio. She had already survived an ambush with him. They also knew about the fact that she once dated a mobster herself. And they all knew Alexio, for all of his disagreements with them, would never place the family in any jeopardy by bringing just anybody around them. She was somebody, they all understood, that Alexio trusted.

Besides, it wasn't as if they could object. Alexio said she could hear it all, then she was going to hear it all. End of discussion. That was the way it was with Alexio: if he wanted it to be a certain way, it was that way. Even back in the day, when Alexio was in the syndicate, Elasaid always, but always, deferred to him.

This time was no different.

"We're at war," Elasaid said to his eldest offspring.

Alex had already figured that much out. War, like pollution, was in the air all around the place.   "With whom?" he asked, not even bothering to look his father's way.

To Alex's surprise, his father didn't respond. Alex looked at him. "With whom?" he asked again.

"With everybody," Oz responded.

Even Kari was shocked to hear that response. She looked at Oz.

Alex, however, looked at his uncles first, who both ranked higher than Oz, and then at his father. "What is that supposed to mean?" Alex asked him.

"It means what he said," responded Elasaid. "We are at war."

"With everybody?"

Elasaid nodded. "Yes."

Alex couldn't believe it. He was surprised, but not shocked. "What did you do?" he asked his father.

But Elasaid was suddenly defensive. "Why would you ask me that, Alexio? Why are you always so judgmental? I did nothing wrong! I have a family to protect. While you are off in America sowing your wild oats, I'm here protecting the family! I did nothing wrong!"

"What did you do, Father?" Alex asked again.

Elasaid still wouldn't respond.

But Jabari would. "He called for the elimination of the heads of the families," he said.

It was Alex's time to be shocked. He looked at his uncle. "He *what*?"

"He called for the elimination of the heads of the families," Maximus said. "And took them all out."

In the Greek Mafia, there were six prominent families. The head of the food chain was the Drakos crime family, a family known for its unusual viciousness in an already vicious game. But it wasn't a blowout. All the other families ranked just beneath them.

Alex first looked at Oz. "You went along with this?" he asked him.

But Oz said nothing. He just stared at his father.

Alex looked at his father, too. He knew he could be ruthless, but this was taking it to an entirely different level. "You ordered the elimination of all five leaders of the families?" he asked his father.

"I had no choice, did I?" his father responded with an edge in his voice. "What else was I supposed to do? Let them muscle me out? Let them make me irrelevant in an underworld I created?! What the fuck was I supposed to do?"

Elasaid had to calm down. His wife even placed her hand over his hand. She was worried about him.

Then he continued on. "After I took out the heads, I assumed they would come to me. That's the way it's done in our country. How was I to know that they would combine forces as one against me? How was I to know that instead of coming to me, they were coming *for* me?"

Alex just sat there. Kari could see his jaw tightened, and his entire body go into that tense place where rage bubbled just beneath the surface.

Then finally, Alex spoke. But his look was just as perplexed as it was angry. "Why would you do such a thing, Papa?" he asked him, calling him the name his siblings still called their father. "Why would you put your family in this kind of harm's way?"

"I had no choice!" Elasaid said again. "They were attempting to muscle me out. Me!"

"Muscle you out of what?" Alex asked. A fixed frown was on his troubled face. "Territory?"

"If only it was that simple," said his father.

"Then what is it?" Alex asked.

Oz spoke up. "They made an attempt to bribe officials and muscle Papa out of the profits from the upcoming International Games. They will be held in Greece for the first time in decades. Every family was clamoring to get their piece of the pie. The other five families tried to take our piece, too."

"You see?" Elasaid asked. "What choice did they give to me? If they would have removed my shot at all contracts, where would we be as a family? If I allowed them to take me out of contention, then what relevancy would I have? It would be a feeding frenzy on us! Everybody would challenge me. We wouldn't stand a chance of survival! I had to do what I did."

"But all five heads?" Alex asked. "If there is a challenge to your authority, you take out one. One should be enough. If not, then another one. That would send the message loud and clear. But you took out *all* of them? The only message that could send is war. Total war!"

Then a voice came over the home's emergency intercom system. All calls were screened at the front gate before they could be dispatched to the family home. It was the security chief. "Sir," he said in a hurried voice, "a call just came in that you must hear."

The family all looked at Elasaid. He must hear it? It had to be serious. "Dispatch it through," Elasaid ordered.

As soon as the call was dispatched through, all that could be heard was screaming. The blood curling screams of Zylena Drakos!

"*Papa, voithiste me!*" she cried over the phone. (*Papa, help me!* she cried over the phone). Every man at the table jumped to their feet. It was only then did Kari actually realize that Zylena wasn't at the dinner table.

"*Oi oikogeneies me piran!*" Zylena was screaming. (*The families took me*, Zylena was screaming). "*Voithiste me! Voithiste me! Voithiste me, Papa!*" (*Help me! Help me! Help me, Papa!*)

"Where is she?" Oz urgently asked his mother.

"She said she was staying in for tonight," said her mother. "At her villa. But you know how Zee sneaks out to be with those boys."

All of the men, including Alex, ran out of the dining hall.

Kari was about to rise to go with them, but Leda sat her back down. "You must wait here," she said to Kari, her face now showing her distress.

"Where are they going?" Kari asked. She was distressed too.

"To track her," said Leda. "And no woman is allowed in the tracking room."

Kari found it strange that a man like Alex would be a party to a *no-women-allowed* room, but what did she expect? Alex had already warned her, before they even arrived in Greece, that his family was not as good as the

Brady Bunch family. But after what she heard at that dinner table, and what the father admitted to doing right in front of her, the Brady Bunch her foot. These people weren't even as good as the Manson family!

She sat back down.

CHAPTER THIRTY

The tracking room was a giant GPS-styled system that Elasaid had installed to keep tabs on his entire family. He got behind the desk and, with Alex, Oz, and his brothers at his side, pulled up Zylena's file.

"It shows that she did leave the castle grounds," Elasaid noted as he checked out the co-ordinances. "Then to a club."

"Which means she left of her own free will," said Oz.

"But her car is still there," responded Elasaid.

"Which club?" Jabari asked.

"*Thyella*," responded Elasaid.

Oz immediately pressed the intercom button. "Get a team to *Thyella*. Zylena's car is there. Tear that place upside down in search of her."

"Yes, sir!" the security chief responded.

"What about her phone?" asked Alex.

"I'm searching it now," responded his father.

"Is it at the club, too?" asked Oz.

"It moved from the club, but only a few meters. That is where it lays."

"Undoubtedly tossed there," said Maximus.

Elasaid nodded. "The only answer. The location is in the middle of the street."

"Any other way to track her?" Alex asked.

"No," said Elasaid. "Unfortunately, no!"

Then they all looked at Alex. Back in the day, when he ran things, he would be the one to come up with the clever answers. Everybody knew what had to be done to get Zylena back, but Alex wasn't sharing his opinion.

It was Elasaid who stood up. "We waste time," he said. "I've got to meet with the families, in exchange for them handing over Zee."

"But which family has her?" Oz asked. "We know next to nothing at this point, Papa."

"And you are the last one who can agree to meet with them," said Maximus. Then he looked at his oldest nephew. "Only Alexio can do that," he said.

"Alexio?" asked Elasaid.

"Yes," Jabari agreed with their brother. "Alexio is the only one they still respect. He is the only one they know had no hand in the dirty deed. They will murder you on sight, Elasaid."

Alexio knew it was true, just as all of them knew it was true, but he remained silent. The Greek mafia, he knew, was the very definition of a slippery slope. Once you get on that slide, you can only go down, and down so far in the mud that you are more than likely to get stuck.

But then the phone rang and took the decision out of his hands.

The call was dispatched through by security without prompting Elasaid because, apparently, he knew who was on the other line. Unlike the first call, where the screaming obscured the voice, there was no question of the voice on this call.

It was Batebbi, the underboss of the Galen crime family. And his message was clear: "We have the girl," he spoke in Greek. "Bring

Elasaid to us," he added, "and we will release her unharmed. Refuse, and she dies."

Elasaid was about to respond, but Alex held up his hand. And Alex, to the delight of everyone in the tracking room, responded. "Your demand is not reasonable," he said.

"Who is this? Is this who I think it is?"

"It is Alexio, Batebbi. You have my sister."

"Ace is back! Well. I did not anticipate such turn of events."

Neither did Alex! "We have to call a truce," Alex said. "Because, you know, if you kill my father, I will have to take action against you. What good will that do any of us?"

"There was a truce. You people leave us alone, we leave you alone. But the truce was broken by your father!"

"I will meet with you. You make your demands. And I will bring them back to my father."

"And if he refuses our demands?" asked Batebbi.

"If they are reasonable," Alex said, "you have my word he will not refuse to comply."

Oz looked at his father. Nobody on the face of this earth could speak so assuredly for him as Alex could. It was that very strength that allowed Oz to be in awe of his big brother, and to despise his big brother too.

"But first," Alex added, "you must release Zylena."

There was a long pause, as, Alex was certain, Batebbi was conferring with the others. Then he was back on the phone. "You will come alone?" he asked Alex.

"To negotiate a truce? Will you come alone?"

Batebbi laughed. "The same old Ace! Okay. You bring three with you. You may bring one other to take your sister away. But no others. We had been playing based on your father's terms. Now they are our terms."

"Agreed," Alex said.

"When?"

Alex looked at his father. Elasaid mouthed the word *now* emphatically.

"Now," said Alex. "In a neutral location."

And the meeting that Elasaid had been hoping for all along, especially after his disastrous decision, was set.

CHAPTER THIRTY-ONE

Alex walked Kari to their villa and closed the door behind them. She could see the strain on his face, and it was a different kind of stress than she'd ever seen on him before. It looked as if the weight of the world was on his shoulders, and the weight of being responsible for her as well. And she knew, in that moment, that Alex was back in the game.

"This was not the way I envisioned this trip would be," he said to her.

"What are you planning to do?"

"After they release Zee, then Oz and I, along with our two uncles, are going to meet with the families," he said.

Terror gripped Kari and she was about to speak her concerns, but Alex placed his finger to her lips. "It is non-negotiable, honey," he said. "I have no choice in this matter."

"The same way your father had no choice in what he did?" Kari asked.

"In this world, as you know how it was in Vito Visconni's world, yes. The same way my father believed he had no choice."

Kari gripped his shirt. "But it's dangerous, Alex." She said this with pain in her big, brown eyes.

Alex smiled a smile that produced wrinkles on the side of his tired blue eyes. "Nothing will happen to me," he said. "These men I know. What my father did was unconscionable, but what they tried to do was unconscionable too."

Kari frowned. "What did they try to do? Squeeze him out of profiting from those upcoming International Games?"

"They are almost as big as the Olympics," Alex said. "The money they generate will be enormous. If the Drakos family does not participate, my father is right: they will be challenged and ultimately eliminated. He had to set them straight."

"I understand something had to be done. But all of them, Alex?"

Alex frowned and shook his head. "It was a terrible decision. An awful decision." Then he exhaled. "But it's done now. And all I can do is get my sister back and try as hard as I can to agree to terms that will diminish my family's standing in the underworld, but will not put them at any more risk than they already are."

Kari studied his face. "You feel you owe them that much?"

Alex shook his head. "I don't owe them shit. But Odysseus did not launch such an elaborate scheme to get me here for no reason. He knew, as I know, that I am their only hope of survival. I have to negotiate a truce. That is the least I can do."

"And if your father won't accept it?" Kari asked.

"He'll accept it."

"But if he won't, Alex?"

"Then he will die. He'll accept it."

Kari nodded. But still she hated that Alex had to do their bidding!

Alex placed his hands on her arms. "I brought you here so that you could get an unvarnished view of who you are interested in being with," he said. "I needed you to know every side of me. The good side, which you and Jordan helped to bring to the forefront, but also the bad and the ugly sides, too. Greece contains the bad and the ugly sides. You had to see this to decide if you can live with a man with this side, too."

"How long before you have to leave?" Kari asked.

It was an odd question to ask after Alex had exposed his inner thoughts to her, at least from his perspective. "The meeting won't be for another couple hours. But I'll need to prepare."

"Then I need to ask you something," Kari said.

"Ask away," Alex said. "You have my undivided attention."

"It may be a crazy time to bring it up."

"Welcome to my world," Alex said with a smile. "Crazy is normal in my world. So whatever your question is, it will fit right in."

Kari smiled too. "I was brought up in a rough part of Miami," she said. "My father was a drug dealer. I hooked up with a made man in the mob. I know what this life can be like. Maybe not on this scale, but I know the life. But I don't know what this is."

Alex was confused. "What *what* is?" he asked.

"Us, Alex. You and me. I've never been in a relationship like this. You brought me into this world to see if I'm hard enough to take it, but we haven't even discussed where we stand. I don't know where this is headed. I don't even know if we have an exclusive relationship right now."

Alex nodded and squeezed her arms. "I thought, after that referendum passed in Florida and I was granted the right to build my casino and hotel, there would be a settling down period for us to talk about our relationship and how we wanted to proceed. But then those assassination attempts changed the equation again, and caused me more distraction. But we'll talk, Karena. I promise you that."

"If we were to become exclusive," Kari said, "and I'm not saying we are now, but if we were to become exclusive, are there many?"

"Many what?"

"Are there many women you'll need to have a conversation with."

Alex hesitated before responding. Then he responded. "Not as many as the tabloids would have you believe," he said. "But yes."

Kari felt a jolt of reality slink through her body. Alex was all but saying, in so many words, that they were moving toward that totally exclusive relationship, but he also seemed to suggest that they weren't there yet. But why was he bringing her here, and exposing his entire other side to her? Was he trying to make sure she was tough enough first?

But then he reached into his pocket, pulled out a loaded revolver, and handed it to Kari. He knew she was tough. But could she survive his family? "While I'm gone," he said, "I want you to keep it with you at all times. Trust no one. Open this door for no one but me. I don't care if my father bangs this door down, you aim it as if you plan to use it, you hear me? While I'm gone, it's your job to keep yourself alive."

Kari thought about Jordan. "Don't worry," she said.

Alex nodded too. "I know I can depend on you, Kari. No harm will come to you, but I don't want to take any chances."

Kari grabbed his shirt lapel. "You listen to me, Alexio Drakos. You don't be in that meeting worrying about me. I can take care of myself. I survived Vito's bullshit, remember?"

Alex smiled.

"I know I can survive your family's." Then she frowned. "I need you to survive them," she said. "I need you to survive that meeting."

A surge of emotion overtook Alex, and he pulled Kari into his arms. He had so much baggage to clean up to be with this woman that it seemed daunting no matter how he looked at it. She didn't know the half of that part of his life! He still was certain she didn't know what she was getting into, and if he was half the man he ought to be he would have not allowed her to get involved with him at all. But he already felt as if he was too far gone. This early, and he already felt that way. But one thing he knew for certain: Kari Grant was tough enough. He was certain she was up for the challenge.

He continued to hold her, even after he knew it was time to get ready.

CHAPTER THIRTY-TWO

Two cars pulled up at the designated location: a poolhall in the fishing village of Argostoli. It was surrounded with security, an army of security, as the cars came to a stop.

The first car was driven by Cronos, Alex's security chief while he was in Greece, and Alex and Oz sat in the backseat. The second car, with one of Alex's men driving and one riding shotgun, contained Jabari and Maximus in their backseat. But as soon as the two vehicles drove up, the muscle for the Galen clan, who had been waiting out front, walked over.

"No security allowed inside," said one of the men.

Alex already knew the drill. He looked at Cronos, who knew the drill too. Cronos nodded, and Alex and Oz got out.

With their uncles out of the second car, the four Drakos men were escorted to a back room inside the empty pool hall and told to wait. It was a risk, and all four men knew it, but Alex also knew there was no other way around it. The respect he had with the families was the only weapon he could use if his own family, thanks to his father's savagery, was to be preserved.

But when the door opened, and the five underbosses of the five crime families walked in, Alex, Oz, and their uncles rose in respect, although Alex could see the hatred in their eyes.

Alex also saw that Batebbi, the underboss of the Galen clan, was now the appointed leader of all five families, when he sat down first. Alex and his team sat down second. And then the rest of the men.

"You brought Cronos and his crew with you," Batebbi said in Greek.

"They're outside," said Alex. "They won't interrupt unless they have to."

"Was that the deal we agreed upon?" Batebbi asked. "You know it is not. But it is always like a Drakos man to change the terms."

"To cheat," said another underboss.

Alex did not even look his way. Batebbi was in charge. "No change in terms," he said.

"You have security outside. Considerable security. We have only a few men outside, too."

"But we have the upper hand now. We have your sister."

Alex's jaw tightened. "You release her first, and then we discuss the truce. That was the agreement."

Anger appeared in Batebbi's eyes. "Your father killed my father," he said. "Your father killed all of our fathers. All five! And you want to sit up here and tell me about an agreement? We discuss the truce," he declared, "and then, if the terms are what we can accept, she will be released."

Alex stared at him. Thanks to his father they were in no position to bargain, and he knew it. "What will be required for a truce," Alex asked.

"Complete and total surrender. You give us your father. Then there will be peace."

"What will be required for a truce?" Alex asked again.

"You do not even consider my terms," said Batebbi. "What did you think I was going to say? Your father broke the peace. He broke it in a way that could have destroyed us all. But we, the number twos, pulled together. We refused to let that bastard win." Then he added: "We shocked the shit out of him, in American jargon. Now we are more powerful than he thought he would become when he first tried to cheat us."

"Cheat you?" Oz asked. "What are you talking about, Batebbi? Our father did not cheat you. It was you who tried to cheat us."

Batebbi smiled. "Is that what he told you?"

"Tell us what you mean," Alex said.

"The war began," Batebbi said, "because your father, Elasaid Drakos, decided to muscle all of us out of the profits from the International Games that are coming to Greece."

Alex just sat there. His father had said they muscled him out of the profits!

But Batebbi continued. "We cannot allow one man to dominate all of us. We will cease to exist as individual corporations if your father has his way. We are a democracy in the Greek underworld. We will not allow a dictator like your father to overthrow us."

Alex's mind was in overdrive. What was his father up to? Why did he lie about them muscling him out of the profits, when it was the other way around?

"Are you alright, Alexio?" Batebbi asked. "You look unwell!" The underbosses laughed.

Then Batebbi turned serious. "When the heads of our families agreed to join forces to stop your father, he agreed to meet with them to negotiate. There was plenty of money to go around. There was no need for this power grab by your father. So they met. All six heads of the families. And it was then did your father, and men he had somehow smuggled in, took the other five leaders out."

Everything sounded sideways. Alex had to think the way his father would think. Why would he tell such lies? Why would he claim what wasn't true? Then Alex understood why. His father told the lies he told to get Alex to set up a meeting. He told such lies so that Alex could arrive at the meeting, find out the truth, and then what? Take them out? But why would he think Alex would do such a thing? These men knew and trusted Alex. They knew his word was his everything. Why would he sacrifice that trust by getting into a gun battle with all five underbosses and, while he was at it, their men outside? Elasaid had to know that Alex didn't operate that way.

Unless, Alex thought, and then he realized how his father's twisted mind would set this up. He jumped from the table, turning toward his uncles, just as both Jabari and Maximus, his uncles, pulled out their weapons and shot one and then another underboss, and was about to kill a third one. But the three other bosses pulled their weapons, too, forcing Alex and Oz to pull theirs.

But Alex, shocking every one, pointed his gun, not at the bosses, but at his uncles. "Drop it!" he ordered them. "They have Zylena! What are you doing?" The plot was crystal clear to Alex now. His uncles were in it with his father. They wanted countrywide domination, and they needed Alex to get them through the door to make it happen fast: with a take out of the five underbosses the same way his father had taken out the bosses.

But as a testament, Alex felt, to just how poorly thought out his father's plan actually was, the door of the room flung open and the Galen men ran in. The sound of the gunfire was why they came. The sound of the gunfire was why they came ready to shoot first.

Now it was a fight for survival. Those uncles didn't give a damn that Zylena was being held hostage. They just wanted that power. They just wanted their brother, Alex's father, to dominate the entirety of the underworld. Alex and Oz had to dive to avoid certain death.

No longer could any truce be reached. No longer could there be any negotiated settlement. It was each man for himself. And Alex, on his back, shot back. He shot and killed every man pointing in his direction. It was agonizing, but he shot and killed Batebbi, and another underboss, and the final one. Alex would have killed every man in that room to stay alive!

Oz, along with the uncles, were shooting too, killing as many of that first wave of men who had entered that room.

When the last man fell, Jabari yelled, "this way!" and Alex, Oz, and Maximus hurriedly followed him out of a side door that led down a long corridor. Alex was on his wrist microphone. "We're heading toward the south side of the building. The south side. Don't come in. Ambush. Don't come in!" He was warning Cronos and his men. Meet them on the south end of the building, he was telling them. They wouldn't stand a chance inside.

And he was right. He was right because as soon as they hit the corridor, the second wave of shooters had arrived, and they were running down the corridor, too, firing as they ran. If Jabari had not found a side room for them to duck into, they all would have been dead.

They ducked into that room, with Alex having to dive in. But they knew they had to come back out shooting. They couldn't wait for those gunmen to block them in.

Alex didn't hesitate. Like the old days, Alex reappeared in that corridor firing before he showed his face, and his brother and uncles followed his lead. They took out as many as they could, and avoided being hit themselves, but the second wave of men was larger than the first wave. It was too many men. The only thing they had going for them was the fact that they were in front.

Taking advantage of their head start, they took off further down the corridor, around another corridor, until they were running toward, and then opening, a backdoor.

To their relief, Cronos had heeded Alex's warning and drove, along with the second car behind him, to the southside of the building and was waiting there.

Jabari and Maximus jumped into the first car. Alex and Oz jumped into the second car. And as the second wave of gunmen ran out of that building firing shot after shot with a vengeance, the two cars sped away. Outracing bullets.

CHAPTER THIRTY-THREE

Kari, with that loaded gun still in her hand, stood at the floor-to-ceiling window inside Alex's childhood bedroom, or *villa* as the Drakos's referred to it, when she heard a hard knock on the door.

"Miss Grant?"

It was Alex's father.

Kari stood erect. "Yes?"

"Open the door, please. It's about Alexio."

Kari began to move closer to the door. "What about Alex?" she asked.

"Open the door, please, and I will tell you. It is not good news, I am sad to say. He told me to come and get you." More knocks. "Open the door, please. It is not safe here!"

Kari's heart was hammering. Every muscle in her body was telling her to run to that door and open it. What if Alex was hurt? What if Alex needed her?

More knocks. "Miss Grant, please open the door so that I may explain to you what has just transpired."

She heard what Alex's father was saying, but she remembered what Alex had said. She was not to open that door for anybody but him. He didn't care who was on the other side. Do not open that door!

She began running, as if her life depended on it, across the massive bedroom toward the bathroom door.

Just as she did, she heard Elasaid say "do it," and then she heard kicks on that bedroom door. Then the door was kicked in. The men who kicked the door open came in first, but Elasaid was right behind them. And he saw Kari just as she was running toward the bathroom.

"Get that bitch!" Elasaid yelled angrily, and his men ran toward the bathroom, too.

Kari could feel them closing in as they ran at an angle, putting them almost at the same distance from that bathroom as she was. One of Elasaid's men was even able to reach out and grab Kari's blouse, and was about to sling her away from that bathroom door and into their clutches. But Kari snatched away from him, entered the bathroom, and slammed that door shut. Then she quickly locked it.

She held up that loaded gun Alex had given to her with trembling hands, backing away from that door in a state of pure panic, as the men on the other side began kicking it in. She was going to have to kill them. She was going to have to kill each and every one of those motherfuckers who tried to come for her. Before, when she was in this position, Alex was with her. Her protector was protecting her. Now she was all alone.

But then she remembered something else Alex had told her. It was during a conversation they had at that window overlooking the sea. Alex said he would go to that sea, late at night, through an escape route *"behind the sink in the bathroom of this very villa, a passage that my parents did not know existed. I happened upon it by accident myself."*

Kari quickly looked at that sink as that door was within a hair's breadth of being kicked down. She pulled on the sink. She tried to push it side to side. But it was a sink! How could Alex claim a sink moved???

Kari was beyond panicking. "Lord, help me," she was crying. "I don't know where. Where, Lord, where?!"

But the men outside of that bathroom door weren't waiting for answers. They leaned back one last time, and kicked it all the way down. They ran into that sizeable bathroom, and Elasaid ran in behind them.

To their shock, there was no Kari. They looked up and down. Around and around. But the black girl was gone.

"Impossible!" Elasaid said. There were no hiding places in that bathroom. There were no corners or moveable objects. And they all saw her go into this place!

Then Elasaid looked up. There was an air vent on the side wall. It didn't look wide enough to him, nor did it look as if it had been tampered with. But that was all they had!

"Remove that vent and see if she somehow got in there," he ordered to the crew chief. "And get men to surround the castle in search of her. I want her found."

"Dead or alive?" the chief asked him.

"Dead or alive!" Elasaid replied, and angrily left the bathroom.

His plan had gone awry already, he thought, as he left. She was going to be his hostage. She was going to be that extra leverage he had should Alexio try something crazy. Because Elasaid knew his son. He knew he was going to make it out alive with those five underbosses no matter who didn't make it. Alexio, he was certain, would.

And he just might come for his father.

But when Elasaid was angry, he was irrational. And he was irrational now. He didn't care about having a hostage. He didn't care about having a bargaining chip. He just wanted that bitch captured, however way they caught her.

CHAPTER THIRTY-FOUR

"What the fuck was that about?" Alex yelled at his kid brother as Cronos sped their car away from that poolhall in Argostoli.

"How the fuck should I know?" Oz yelled back. "I didn't know this was going to happen! My job was to get you back in Greece to negotiate a truce because you're the only one they would meet with. They were supposed to release Zylena, and we were supposed to negotiate a truce!"

"Zylena!" Alex said, his heart heavy. "How could Jabari and Maximus come out firing when they knew those bastards had our sister? Their asses weren't there to negotiate any truce. Their asses were there to take Batebbi and all of the others out." Then Alex hit the side of the door panel and yelled, "motherfuckers," so violently that Cronos glanced at him through the rearview mirror, to make sure he was going to be alright.

Then Alex had another thought, about another woman, and he pulled out his cellphone.

"And what was that shit about Papa muscling them out of the Games," Alex asked Oz, "when Papa said they had muscled him out? Batebbi told the truth about that too?"

He could tell Oz hated to admit it. But he admitted it. "Yes," he said.

Alex shook his head. How could he have not seen this? How could he have allowed himself, and his good name, to get mixed up in this backward-ass bullshit?!

"But we were still there to negotiate a truce," Oz said. "And to get Zylena back. We've got to get to the castle, and see if they will be willing to reason with us and return her unharmed. That's our only option. They have to know that father has the upper hand now, no matter how he got it. He is firmly in control now. Their second-tier leaders are now dead too. Thanks to you," Oz added, which only angered Alex more. "Father now is the sole leader of the Greek Mafia. But if you're asking me if I knew Jabari and Maximus were going to pull that shit, Alex, before we even had Zylena's release, the answer is no. You know I would not have approved anything that nuts. I had no idea."

Alex could kill somebody right now! He was that upset. But he called Kari instead. She was in that house with that twisted, power-hungry motherfucker. He had to make sure she was okay.

But Oz was frowning. "What are you doing?" he asked him.

"Calling Karena," he said.

Oz stared at his big brother as if he was staring at a stranger. At a time like this he was worried about a lady? Alexio? The man with a lady for every day of the week? For every mood he was in? Was this man *his* big brother?

But Kari didn't answer the call. And it terrified Alex. "Faster, Cronos," he said to his driver. "Get me back to the castle as fast as this bucket can get me there!"

And Cronos floored the gas, and flew right past the car in front: the car containing Alex's uncles.

Kari had gotten out. Just when she prayed, and needed that sink to do for her what it did for Alex, she felt around to the furthest underside of the sink, found a button, and pressed it hard. The sink slid open to a passageway, and she ran through it. As she was pulling the sink back closed, Elasaid men had kicked the door down.

Now she was running. And if she doubted it before, she did not doubt it now: she was running for her life.

But it was tricky. She had to scale down the side of a mountain. But she did it. She hurried down rock after rock after rock until she was near the bottom. But when she saw at the bottom, a group of Elasaid's men seemingly searching for her, she started running sideways, toward the plateau of woods that ran parallel to the sea. But someone on the ground saw her, and began firing.

She darted into those woods and kept running. She had one loaded gun. She was not going to be able to outshoot an army of men. She ran.

But just as she was nearing a clearing, and was about to take it, another group of men, this time two of them, were seen. When she saw them, they saw her, and they attempted to get off a round. But Kari dropped back and fired first, and fired repeatedly. She hit them both.

But she knew the sound of the bullets had alerted that other group of men, the larger group, and she had to keep running!

She ran across the clearing, back into another thicket of woods, and kept on running. What she loved about Alex was the level of confidence he had in her abilities. He truly believed she could handle situations like this. What she hated most about Alex was his confidence in her abilities. She wasn't at all sure if she could handle shit! But she knew she had to. Not just for her own sake. Or even Alex's. But for Jordan's sake. Nobody was going to take care of him the way she did. No matter how bleak it looked now, she was going home to her son.

But it only got bleaker. As soon as Kari made her way out of those woods, and was hopeful that she had strayed far enough away from the larger group of men, she found herself face to face, not only with yet another group of men, but their pointed rifles too. All sixteen of them.

She dropped her own weapon, and held up her hands.

CHAPTER THIRTY-FIVE

The gates to the castle were quickly opened, and the two cars, led by Cronos's car, sped inside. Alex and Oz jumped out of the car, and ran into the main house. They did not wait for their uncles to so much as open a car door. They knew who was the boss. They knew that Jabari and Maximus did not fart without Elasaid giving them permission.

And Elasaid, along with his wife Leda, were waiting in the living room. Oz ran up to his father. Alex, however, ran up the stairs. He had to check on Kari first!

"How could you, Papa?" Oz asked. "They still have Zylena!"

Leda was angry. "You left her? How could you leave without her?"

"What are you talking about, Mother? There was no choice to be had! Jabari and Maximus came out shooting. They did not give us a chance to get her out. They did not give us a chance to negotiate a truce! They did not give us a chance!"

Upstairs, Alex heard his family's voicing, arguing the way they usually did, but his mind was focused on getting Kari. He ran all the way around that wing of the home until he made it to his bedroom. When he saw that the door had been kicked open, his heart dropped. "Kari?" he yelled as he ran into the bedroom. But Kari was nowhere to be found. And when he saw that the bathroom door in the back of the room had been not only kicked open, but kicked all the way down, his heart fell. He ran into that bathroom, praying there would be no blood. There was none.

And then he looked at the sink.

Kari, he was pleased to see, had attempted to push it all the way back in place. And she almost succeeded. No man, who did not know better, would have seen the inch of space between the sink and the wall. But Alex saw it. And it was the first time since the madness began did he begin to feel hopeful.

But that hope was crushed as soon as he was about to run to that sink and go and find her. Oz ran into the room.

"Alex! Alex!" he yelled.

Alex turned around.

"Papa has Karena."

What did he mean by Papa *having* Karena? He spoke as if she was his prisoner. But Alex did not ask for clarification. He hurried past his brother, and then they both hurried downstairs.

Kari was standing in the living room with two of Elasaid's men holding her by her arms. There was now a large army of Elasaid's men in the living room. They had found Kari, and all had come in together. Jabari and Maximus had arrived in that living room too.

But as Alex came down those stairs and saw her standing there, he was livid. "Release her at once!" he yelled angrily to those men. "Remove your hands from her!"

But both men looked at Elasaid. And Alex began to make a fast run toward Kari, to release her himself, but every man in Elasaid's army of men closed in on him with their weapons trained at his head. It was only then did Alex understand just how different everything had become. He used to command every one of those men, and they respected his command. Now he was just another enemy Elasaid ordered them to dislike.

Alex looked at Kari. She tried to smile, to let him know that she was okay, but he could see that look of terror in her eyes. But he knew what he had to do. His only purpose was getting Kari out of this country, and his father's house, alive.

"Let her go, Papa," Oz said to their father. "Why have you captured her."

"I thought I could use her," Elasaid. "For leverage. But you and your brother performed mightily. Especially you, Alex. I ordered Odysseus to bring you here to get us in that meeting room with all five number twos. You did that for us." He smiled. "You even killed them for us, from what I'm understanding from my brothers," he added. "That is all I need from you. Now I dominate this country. Now they will have no choice but to come to me."

"And what about Zylena?" Alex said. "Or do you not care?"

"I care," Elasaid said. "A little."

"Elasaid!" Leda yelled at him in horror. "Do not speak so cavalier of your own daughter!"

"I care," Elasaid said again, "but I care about our position in this country more. They will do her no harm because they know I am now in charge. They will have to come to me. Everything comes through me now!"

Alex looked at Kari. "Are you alright?" he asked her.

"She's fine," Elasaid replied before Kari could. "I ordered them to kill her if they had to," he added. "And they would have had she not been so black." His brothers laughed. "They simply could not see her!"

Alex made an aggressive move toward his father. He just wanted to get his hands on that bastard. But Elasaid men stopped him, with their weapons and their hands. He, too, was now their prisoner.

But then the phone rang. It had been dispatched straight through by Security.

Everybody looked at Elasaid. He nodded at Jabari.

Jabari walked over to the phone, placed it on Speaker, and then spoke. "We have Zylena," the voice on the other end said.

"And we have the power," Jabari responded. "Which of those, do you suppose, are more potent?"

There was a long pause on the other end of the line. "We are willing to negotiate a truce," he said.

Elasaid grinned, and shoved a fist in the air. He mouthed, "I knew it," as he did.

Jabari looked at him. "They want to negotiate a truce now," he said with his own cocky smile.

But Elasaid quickly shook his head. "No truce. They have no power against me. But they may join me."

"Tell them not to harm Zylena, Elasaid," Leda insisted.

"No harm," Jabari said to the voice on the other end of the line, "has come to Zylena?" he asked.

"No harm yet," said the voice.

"Harm her and you die," Jabari said. "We will call you back with our terms." And he ended the call.

"You bastard!" Oz yelled at Jabari. "You could have ordered them to bring Zylena home. You could have pretended to want a truce just to get Zylena home!"

"We'll get her home," Elasaid replied, "but only on our terms. When they took her, they did us a good turn. They forced Alex to make a decision to meet with them much faster than I had anticipated. They can keep her a little longer."

"And you," Elasaid added, "can take your whore and get out of my country. Your usefulness is now beyond its sell-by date. Leave and do not come back."

The men finally removed their guns from Alex's head, and the two men removed their hands from Kari's arms. Kari ran toward Alex, and Alex ran to Kari. And he did not delay. He did not look at his mother, his father, nor his own brother. He took Kari in his arms, and left that house as quickly as his feet could take him. He did not look back.

Cronos drove Alex and Kari along the winding driveway that led to the security gate. And when the gate opened, and gave them safe passage out, Cronos drove along the side of the private road that surrounded the castle. But it drove slowly. Very slowly. Kari knew something more was up.

She looked at Alex. Still holding her hand, he turned to her. "I want you to go to the plane," he said. "Cronos will see you safely there. You can trust him."

"What are you going to do?" Kari asked him with grave reservations in her voice.

"What I should have done a long time ago," Alex responded. But he would not say more.

Kari stared in his hard, blue eyes. "You may need backup, Alex."

"No."

"Whenever I'm with you," Kari said, "I have no fear. I know I'll be okay. You may need backup, Alex."

Alex stared at her. How could he allow her to go into such a dangerous situation? But what if they attacked her at the plane? What if

Cronos was unable to protect her? What if something happened to her because she was not in his sight, and at his side?

It was a calculated crapshoot. But he made a decision.

She was safer with him.

He lifted his hand. Cronos saw it. And pulled to the side of the road.

They entered the house the way Kari, at the moment of her gravest danger, exited it: through the passage way behind the bathroom sink. They were armed and ready: both with high-powered shotguns, and both with silencers on the muzzles.

Downstairs, the Drakos family was still in the living room. Jabari and Maximus were having drinks. Oz was slouched down on the couch, still processing what had transpired, and Leda was still arguing with Elasaid about the best way to get their daughter back, and back unharmed. The army of men had now gone, and the castle was back to normal.

As Alex and Kari entered the landing that led to the staircase, they stood at the railing that overlooked the living room.

"Who?" asked Kari.

"Odysseus," replied Alex. "Make sure he remains neutral."

Kari nodded and pointed her weapon in the direction of Oz. And then Alex lifted his shotgun, aimed, and fired. Maximus took a shot to the forehead, and fell first. The silencer did its job, and nobody heard the shot. But they saw Maximus fall.

Especially Jabari, who was suddenly fearful. After all they had survived, had his beloved brother succumbed to some sort of heart attack?

But that was exactly as Alex had wanted it. He wanted Jabari, the ringleader of those two sadistic bastards, to feel pain first. And then Alex shot Jabari, through the side of the head, ending his reign.

When Jabari fell too, Oz jumped up from the couch, and Elasaid looked up at the top of the staircase.

As Kari kept her weapon trained on Oz, Alex trained his weapon on his father. "Move one muscle," he said, "and you're dead."

Elasaid and Leda both, appearing shocked, stared at Alex as they placed their hands in the air.

And Alex and Kari made their way downstairs.

They arrived outside the gate at the Galen estate three hours after the phone call had been made. Even with Alex's small group of men assisting, it took that long because of the way they had to get out of the castle without alerting Elasaid's guards. But they made in two cars. Alex and Kari, driven by Cronos, was in the second car.

Alex released his hand from Kari's, and got out. As soon as he did, the gate was opened and a large army of armed men stood with their weapons aimed. Kari's heart pounded. She grabbed her own weapon, ready to launch a counterattack, but she stared at Alex and waited for a cue from him.

The armed men were led, this time, by the third in command of the Galen crime family. Alex couldn't even remember his name.

But it didn't matter. The guns trained on Alex didn't matter, either. He had a job to do and he was going to finish it.

He went to the first car, opened the back door of the car, and grabbed first Jabari's body, and then Maximus's, and dragged them toward the gate's entrance. He tossed both dead bodies to the feet of the leader.

"These are the men," Alex said, "who attacked you."

"You were there, too," the leader said. "And Odysseus."

"We were defending ourselves. I do not attack when I gave my word I would not."

The leader stared at Alex. Kari could tell that man didn't know what to make of all of this.

But Alex gave him very little time to muse over it. Alex, instead, went back to the first car, opened the front passenger door, and pulled out the prize: his own father, with his hands and feet tied.

All of the men immediately stood at attention. This was amazing if it was true!

But it was true. Alex escorted his own father up to the leader, and pushed him toward them. The leader gladly grabbed him by the arm.

"My sister," Alex said, "for my father. The man who killed all five heads of your families when they thought he came in peace. The man who ordered the killing of all five number twos when I thought we came in peace."

This was the Alexio every man at that gate had heard about, and respected. Alexio Drakos, they were always told, was a man you could always do business with. His word was his life. He would never betray you.

"What is the catch?" the leader asked Alex.

"My sister's release," Alex said again, "and my brother's right to head the Drakos family business. Not as the leader of any one of you, but as an equal."

The leader studied Alex, as if he was considering his response. Then he looked at Elasaid Drakos. They had the king. They had the king!

The leader nodded, and in less than a minute, Zylena came out of the main house, saw her big brother standing there, and began running toward the gate. When she saw her uncles' dead bodies, and her father's tied up body, she hesitated. But then she ran to Alex and fell into his arms. She buried her face in his chest. She had been told how her father, and her uncles, were willing to risk her life for power. She had been told how certain her life was over after the poolhall attack.

And as Alex, with Zylena in his arms, began walking toward the second car, where Kari and Cronos were waiting, Elasaid began to beg. "Alexio, don't do this. Alexio, please, I would have never harmed you. Alexio, these men are going to kill me! They're going to kill me! What did I ever do to you?"

But the gate closed, and Elasaid was now at the mercy of the very families he decimated.

Alex, along with his kid sister, got into the second car. Zylena got into the backseat, leaned against Kari, who placed an arm around her, and cried.

Alex looked at Cronos. Cronos backed up, and drove away.

And Alex Drakos had a sneaking suspicion, a suspicion born out of his heart's desire rather than life's necessity, that he would never see Greece again.

EPILOGUE

They were in the clouds, flying high and away, as they were naked and on their backs, arm in arm, watching the world go by from the comfort of the bedroom onboard. They were in flight, on their way back to Florida, and both were still feeling the sting.

After nearly a half hour of just lying there, Alex finally spoke. "Odysseus phoned me while you were in the tub," he said.

Kari was surprised to hear it. "What did he say?"

"He thanked me. He said the families, what was left of them, called and agreed to a truce."

"But why would they give in if they know they have the upper hand?"

"Because they know they don't," Alex said. "Odysseus has a reputation, too. He is a man who was number two in the largest crime family in Greece. They weren't even number two in their own smaller families. It is in their best interest to do business with Oz."

"And what about your father? What did Oz say about that?"

Alex hesitated. "He didn't," he finally said.

Kari hesitated, and then asked it anyway. "What do you say about that?" she asked.

"I say," Alex said, "you get what you deserve in this life. He killed the bosses, and directed to be killed the underbosses of five organizations. He almost got his own daughter killed. He ordered your execution if his men decided they didn't want to bother bringing you in. What the fuck did he think would be his outcome?"

Kari snuggled against him. "I'm saying," she said.

Then Alex began rubbing her arm. "Thank you," he said.

What was he thinking her for? She looked at him. "For what?"

"For having my back," said Alex. "For not barracking yourself in another room as soon as we boarded this plane. For, hopefully," he added, "deciding not to leave me."

He said those last words with great trepidation. The idea that he would allow himself to be that vulnerable with another human being would have been implausible just a few months ago. Now he felt completely vulnerable with Kari. Completely exposed. But after the way she stepped up for him in Greece, he felt that coming clean and being honest with her was the least he could do.

Kari turned toward him to where her body was halfway on top of his. And she smiled that angelic smile, he thought. "You don't have to thank me again," she said. "I'll glad come to your rescue again and again," she said, and both of them laughed.

But Alex, thrilled beyond measure, slid her body all the way until she was completely on top of him. Then he held her in a big bearhug.

But an hour later, as Kari and Alex both struggled to stay awake, everything turned sideways when Kari's cellphone rang. Alex grabbed it from the nightstand and looked at the Caller ID. "Faye," he said.

Kari took it from him, placed the call on Speaker, and laid back on Alex's chest as she answered the call.   "Faye, hey. Everything alright?"

"Yes, it's. . . You're back in town, right?" she asked.

Kari was puzzled. "Am I back in town? No. Not yet. We're about an hour away. Why?"

There was a pause.   Even Alex looked concerned. "Why, Faye?" Kari asked again.

"It's Jordan."

Kari's heart dropped. She immediately sat up and placed her feet toward the floor, with her ass directly on top of Alex's penis. "What about Jordan?" she asked.

"We can't find him, Kari."

Alex lifted Kari up and stood them both up.

"You can't find him?" Kari was asking, her voice rising with fear.   "What are you talking about you can't find him?"

"We've looked everywhere. We've called everybody he knows. Nobody's seen him, Kari. He was supposed to come home after school. I went to pick him up.   But he wasn't there. Nobody at the school could remember where he went after the bell rung. Nobody's seen him, Kare."

"Check my rental house," Alex said. "He has friends in that neighborhood too."

"Benny checked there already. He checked the pool. The clubhouse. He even checked your house to see if he was around there. He wasn't."

"Oh, God," Kari said. "Oh, God."

"Has this ever happened before?" Alex asked Kari.

"No!" Kari responded. "Never! Jordan always let me know where he is." Then she looked at Alex. "What if it's related to Greece?" she asked. "What if those families . . ."

But Alex was pulling her into his arms. "It's not related, baby. He's not in any danger like that."

But as Kari continued to get information from Faye, Alex moved away from her and called the two security details responsible for Jordan's safety.

But they had no answers, either. Jordan was dropped off at school. They arrived back at the school an hour before the bell rang and waited for him to come out of the school. It was their normal routine, and it had worked every time. Accept this time, they didn't see him. They, in concert with Benny and Faye Church, decided to search for Jordan first, before they made that call. When all else failed, they ordered Faye to make the call.

It wasn't looking good.

And when that plane touched down in Apple Valley, Alex and Kari hit the ground running. Benny and Faye were waiting for them, and Alex knew the two teams of security were out of sight, but waiting too.

Jimmy Hines, Drakos Capital's chief investigator, had been ordered to get to Apple Valley too. Because he was nearby, at his vacation home in Destin, Florida, it worked out. He was able to drive right over and was waiting at the airstrip with the Churches. Alex's G-Wagon was waiting for his use as well.

"Anything?" Kari was asking Faye and Benny as soon as she ran up to them.

"Still nothing, Kari," Benny said. "We've searched everywhere."

"But that's not possible!"

"Four times, Kari," Benny said before she could continue. "We've searched everywhere."

Kari was so distressed that it pained all of them. Faye placed an arm around her. "Jordan is a good kid, Kare," she said. "We'll find him."

But Alex pulled Jimmy Hines aside, and looked at him. "Any leads at all?" he asked him.

Jim shook his head. "It's as if the kid disappeared into thin air. Nobody knows shit."

"One thing I know," Alex said, "is that I want you to pull every member of both details and refresh. Effective immediately."

"Both details?" Jim asked.

"Did I stutter?" Alex asked. "Both, *got*dammit. Both! They should have phoned me when Jordan first turned up missing. That is protocol. If the team leader won't do it, every *got*damn member of the team has to do it. They know the rules. I want every last one of those assholes replaced."

"And fired?"

Alex frowned. It was stressful enough without him playing stupid. He knew how Alex rolled. "Yes, dammit, Jim! What's wrong with you? Yes!"

Then he left Jim's side, and hurried back to Kari. Jim shook his head. It wasn't that he was playing stupid, it was just that he'd never seen his boss this upset over some female or her kid.

The teams split up. Faye and Benny were to not only phone the list of Jordan's friends that they had, but Alex suggested they go to those friends' houses and talk with their parents. See if the parents saw anything. Faye and Benny gladly complied.

Jim and his team were to search around Alex's neighborhood again, and surrounding neighborhoods.

But Alex and Kari went to Kari's house. Faye had already searched there, but Kari wanted to be sure.

When they got there, and found the house not only empty but undisturbed, it was no surprise to either one of them. Just another big letdown. They got back into Alex's car. But Alex waited.

Kari looked at him as if he'd lost his mind. "What are you doing?" she asked him. "Let's go! We've got to find him before it gets dark. Let's go, Alex!"

"Where?" Alex asked.

Kari stared at him. She didn't know where! She just wanted her boy home!

Alex leaned his head back. "We've got to think, Kari."

"I've been thinking. I've been thinking what if it is one of your enemies?"

"It's not," Alex said.

"But it can be."

"No, it can't."

"What about your ex-wife?"

Alex frowned and looked at her. "What? Linda?"

"I heard what Oz said about what you did to her face. She had plastic surgery because of what you did to her. And it was all because of me, wasn't it? And how she disrespected me."

"It was also because I know her. She was not going to let it go."

"See!" Kari said. Alex looked at her. She was too amped-up. "That only proves my point," Kari continued. "She didn't let it go. And decided to hurt my son."

But Alex was shaking his head. "That's not what's happening."

"How can you be so sure?"

Alex looked at Kari. She was beyond distressed, and it hurt him. "While we were still inflight, I had my men track her down. I had them question her with a, let's say, *harsh* interrogation. She is not involved in Jordan's disappearance."

But Kari shook her head. She still wasn't convinced.

"You have got to settle down, honey," Alex said. "You can't think straight in this state of being. He's a smart kid. He's going to be okay. Don't you feel that?"

Kari actually did. "Yes," she said.

"Then let's think about this."

"But what's there to think about, Alex? He's not with any of his friends. Benny is a lawyer. He knows how to question people too. He covered those bases."

"But what if he has a new friend?" Alex asked.

"A new friend?" Then Kari thought about it. "You mean like a girlfriend?"

Alex nodded. "Yes."

"He never mentioned one to me."

"But that doesn't mean he doesn't have one."

Kari agreed. "No, it doesn't." Then she looked at Alex. He was an expert in relationships. "If you were a fourteen-year-old boy, where would you take your girlfriend?"

"This time of day? It's been what, nearly a couple hours after school?" He thought about it.

But then they both looked at each other, and said it simultaneously: "The movies!" they said.

Alex quickly pressed the Start button. "Where's the nearest cinema?" he asked.

"The only cinema," Kari said, "is actually in walking distance of his school!"

Alex smiled. "I'll be damned," he said, and they took off.

And it was as simple as that. Alex and Kari hurried out of the SUV, purchased two tickets to get inside of the cinema, and went from empty theaters to near-empty theaters until they found the right one. It was a long-ass film on World War One and that theater was completely empty. Except for the two young people, Jordan and a beautiful black girl, sitting in the very back of the room. Kissing.

Kari leaned against Alex as a relief filled her entire body. She was going to kill him, but she was so happy he was alright! She was going to kill him, but she was so thrilled that no harm had come to him!

But after the relief washed over her, only anger remained, and she was ready to march up those stairs in that dark theater and embarrass the shit out of Jordan.

But Alex pulled her back. Then pulled her back into the corridor of the movie theater.

Kari looked at him. "What is it?" she asked.

"Jordan has done what most red-blooded American boys do. He's done what I did as a young boy in Greece."

"What's that?" Kari asked.

"He's taking his girl to a movie."

"But no, Alex, no. It's more than that."
Kari's face was sincere and serious. "He could
have told Faye or Benny. They would have let
him go. He didn't have to sneak around and
pull this shit."

"You're right. That was his mistake. But
because we adults overreacted and called in
the Fifth Fleet doesn't make that his mistake
too. He should have told his godparents what
he was doing. Yes, he should have. But let's
not embarrass the boy in front of his girl by
making it more than what it is."

Kari stared at Alex. "I won't make it more
than what it is," she agreed. "But he should
have told Faye and Benny. He knew she was
picking him up from school. He knew they
would worry sick about his whereabouts. And
Jordan knows I don't play like that. He's going
to have to pay for what he put all of us
through."

And Kari left Alex's side, and went into the
theater. Alex was proud of Kari. She stood by
her principles no matter what. If he didn't do
right by her, it was going to be to his own

detriment. He had a lot of old clothes to toss out. A lot of baggage. But she was well worth the effort.

But Alex still felt whimsical. The kid was alright and all was right with his world, too. But he still smiled and raised his eyebrows at just the thought that he couldn't convince Kari to go easy on that little Lover Boy in that theater.

"I tried, Jordan," he said jokingly to no one but himself, as he shook his head and went into the theater too. Kari had his back in the most dangerous of situations. The least he can do, in the most domestic of situations, was to have hers, too.

"I want you to call Aunt Faye and Uncle Benny and personally apologize to those good people who are still running around this town looking for your foolish butt. Then you'll be calling Alex's people too. He's got them all over the place looking. You know better, Jordan. Your ass know better than this!"

Ah, family life, Alex thought delightfully, as he made his way to the back of the theater and sat beside a still-fussing Kari, a terrified young girl, and Jordan, who was listening to his mother's diatribe with big-ass, *I can't believe Mom is back in the country embarrassing the shit out of me*, stunned eyes.

Visit

www.MALLORYMONROEBOOKS.com

or

www.AUSTINBROOKPUBLISHING.com

for more information on all titles.

ABOUT THE AUTHOR

Mallory Monroe is the bestselling author of over eighty novels.
Visit
www.mallorymonroebooks.com
or
www.austinbrookpublishing.com
for more information on all titles.